Careful what you wish for. . . .

"Where are you going, Kane . . . ?"

"I'm supposed to tell you every little detail of my life? I didn't realize that was how this was going to work."

"It's not going to work at all if you keep ditching me to sneak off with some other girl." Miranda sucked in a sharp breath and pressed her hands to her lips. She hadn't been meaning to go that far.

"Stevens . . ." He brushed her hair away from her face and ran his fingers lightly across her lips.

"There's no other girl," he said firmly.

"Then what?"

"It's just not your kind of thing, okay?" he said wearily. "You're going to have to trust me."

"They say every good relationship's built on a fo[und]a- tion of trust," Miranda mused.

"My point exactly."

"So . . ."

"So . . ." he echoed, when she didn't speak.

"So take me with you," she said firmly.

"What about trust?"

"Earn it." Miranda grinned defiantly and, reachi[ng] the steering wheel, rested her hand over his. "And maybe you'll find out you don't know me as well as you think."

Kane's eyes darted toward his watch, and he sighed. "Fine. You want to go, we'll go. But don't say I didn't warn you."

3-14

Carnegie Public Library
101 West Clay
Albany, Missouri 64402

SEVEN DEADLY SINS

Lust
Envy
Pride
Wrath
Sloth
Gluttony
Greed

SEVEN DEADLY SINS

Greed

ROBIN WASSERMAN

SIMON PULSE

New York London Toronto Sydney

This book is a work of fiction. Any references to historical events, real people, or real locales are used fictitiously. Other names, characters, places, and incidents are the product of the author's imagination, and any resemblance to actual events or locales or persons, living or dead, is entirely coincidental.

SIMON PULSE
An imprint of Simon & Schuster Children's Publishing Division
1230 Avenue of the Americas, New York, NY 10020
Copyright © 2007 by Robin Wasserman
All rights reserved, including the right of reproduction in whole or in part in any form.
SIMON PULSE and colophon are registered trademarks of Simon & Schuster, Inc.
Designed by Ann Zeak
The text of this book was set in Bembo.
Manufactured in the United States of America
First Simon Pulse edition July 2007
10   9   8   7   6   5
Library of Congress Control Number 2007923646
ISBN-13: 978-1-4169-0720-6
ISBN-10: 1-4169-0720-3

For Susie

Acknowledgments

This series has added up to more than 1,700 pages, and the full list of people I have to thank could fill every one of them. What follows is a brief excerpt.

All of the credit and none of the blame for everything I've written goes to my amazing editor, Michelle Nagler, who never fails to astonish me.

Bethany Buck has earned every thank-you I've ever given her, and at least a million more. With this series, and with her faith in me, she changed my life.

Caroline Abbey, Amanda Berger, Jennifer Bergstrom, Steve Brezenoff, Robin Corey, Dave Epstein, Jaime Feldman, Emily Follas, Russell Gordon, Nellie Kurtzman, Katie McConnaughey, Robb Pearlman, Michael del Rosario, Orly Sigal, Brenna Sinnott, Simon Tasker, Ann Zeak, and everyone else at Simon Pulse (past and present) have gone above and beyond for these books, every step of the way. They make brilliance look easy.

Erin Downing's creativity and support saved me from at least twelve dead ends. She may even deserve a hug.

Alexis Offen was always there for me, even when she was 3,000 miles away. She should get a medal for her brave and occasionally successful efforts to keep me sane.

Though my parents don't know it, they long ago perfected the art of parenting. They believed I could do anything—but whatever I can do, it's only because of them.

Thanks most of all to Susan Curry, who loved the desert even more than I did. Her friendship made everything possible.

I grant him bloody,
Luxurious, avaricious, false, deceitful,
Sudden, malicious, smacking of every sin
That has a name.
—William Shakespeare, *Macbeth*

All the riches, baby, won't mean anything
All the riches, baby, don't bring what your love can bring.
—Gwen Stefani, "Rich Girl"

chapter

1

"Mirror mirror, on the wall," Beth Manning whispered, "who's the fairest of them all?"

The mirror was silent.

She laughed softly at her own silliness—then froze, realizing that this was the first time in a long time she'd seen a real smile on her face. The girl in the mirror looked unfazed, like smiling was something she did every day. The girl in the mirror, her long blond hair wrapped into an elegant slipknot, her lips brushed a pale pink, her blue eye shadow as shimmery as her strapless blue gown, looked like she didn't have a worry in the world. She looked like the kind of girl who frolicked in enchanted forests, transformed toads into princes, talked to mirrors and expected them to talk back.

She looked happy.

Beth wished the mirror really *was* magical. Because then she could slip into it and hide away. Let her mirror image, the happy girl, the *normal* girl—let that girl go to the prom.

The doorbell rang. Beth drew in a deep breath. She had made her parents promise not to answer it, telling them that she'd spent her whole life picturing the moment where she opened the door to meet her handsome date, Prince Charming come to sweep her away to the ball. She'd made them promise to stay upstairs until called upon, and keep the twins under lock and key so as not to spoil her picture-perfect moment. It was only a half lie.

She *had* spent most of her life picturing this night. She had lain in bed, staring up at the pale pink canopy—the one that was taken down when she got too old, even if, ashamed to admit it, she had wished it could stay forever. The swooping pink fabric made her feel like she was lying down to sleep in some exotic land, a world of silk scarves and magic carpet rides, ladies-in-waiting, Prince Charmings. She had gazed at that canopy, night after night, imagining herself as a high school senior, finally able to escape the dull realities of life in Grace, California, ready to face the world. All grown up.

It'll be fine, she told herself, walking slowly downstairs. This was why she couldn't have her parents in the room. It would take all the strength she had to open the door, to officially begin the night. She wouldn't have anything left over for the artificial smile and the bright tone, the good-daughter act they needed to assure themselves that Beth was still perfect. She needed a moment alone behind the door to close her eyes, breathe deeply, and remember that she was stronger than she looked. She had to be. *I can do this,* she told herself.

The door swung open.

"Whoa. You look . . . whoa."

Beth's throat closed up. She just stood there, staring at the tuxedo, the fresh corsage in its plastic case, the scuffed black loafers, the smoothed-down hair, the black bowtie, impossibly straight. "What are you . . . what are you doing here?"

Reed Sawyer's hands tightened on the corsage case, which crackled as the plastic bent in on itself. His eyes met hers, and, much as she wanted to, she couldn't look away. She'd seen those eyes in her dreams, deep and dark, bottomless. And in her dreams—nightmares, really—they accused her.

But this Reed was real, and there was nothing in his eyes but . . . she wouldn't let herself believe it was tenderness, or affection.

Surely it was just the light.

"I said I'd take you to the prom," he said, his voice the same velvety growl that she remembered. She wanted to touch him. Just his arm, or his shoulder, just to run her fingers lightly across his chest or to straighten the bowtie that didn't need straightening, to reassure herself that he was really there.

"That was last month," she said softly. "Before . . ."

Before he had found out that she was a killer.

It was an accident, she told herself. *I never wanted it to happen.* She was trying to learn to forgive herself. But if it was hard for her to do, it would be impossible for Reed. And why should he want to bother? Reed had only wanted Kaia—and accident or not, Beth had killed her.

"I said a lot of stuff," Reed said.

Beth nodded.

"And I meant it."

Do not *cry,* she ordered herself.

"But . . ." He shrugged. "I said I'd take you to the prom. I keep my promises."

"You went to all this trouble"—Beth gestured at the tuxedo and all of it—"just because . . ." She tucked a loose strand of hair behind her ear. "Reed, you really shouldn't have, I mean—I never would have expected, not after . . ." She took a deep breath and tried to steady herself, or at least steady her voice. "You didn't have to do this."

"I don't do anything because I have to," he reminded her. "But if you want me to go—"

"No!" She reached out for him, then dropped her hand almost as soon as she'd raised it. "Reed, you know how sorry—"

He shook his head. "No more," he said harshly. "You said it enough, and . . ." This time, she had no idea what was hidden in the silence.

And I can't stand to hear it again?

And whatever you say, I'll hate you forever?

And I forgive you?

But he didn't continue, just opened the corsage package and pulled out a single white lily on a thin elastic string. "My dad said I had to get this for you, and since I didn't know what color your dress was going to be, I figured white, so . . ."

"It's beautiful," she told him. "It's perfect." She held out her hand, expecting him to hand her the flower. But instead, he rested his hand beneath her palm and closed his fingers warmly around hers.

Their eyes met again. "Beth, the reason I'm here, the thing is—"

He broke off at the sound of footsteps coming up the walk.

"Beth?" Adam, as always, looked as if he'd been born to wear a tuxedo. He hesitated a few feet away from the doorway, confused.

Reed ripped his hand away. "You're fucking kidding me," he growled, his eyes hardening and his mouth twisting into a scowl. "You work fast, don't you?"

"Reed, wait," Beth pleaded. "We're not together—"

"Lucky him."

"I didn't think you were coming."

"Yeah," Reed snarled. "I got that." He tossed the lily to the ground and turned away. "Forget it." Beth sagged against the door frame, watching him storm down the walkway. *I will not cry,* she told herself. *I will not collapse. I will just—* But she didn't know what she was supposed to do next.

"What was *he* doing here?" Adam asked, hurrying toward the door as if to hold her steady. She waved him away. She couldn't stand the thought of him touching her, not now.

Beth shook her head. "Nothing." The problem was, she didn't *know* what he'd been doing there. "Let's just get out of here."

"Beth, wait." His voice was hesitant, like he was afraid that his next word would set her off. Like she was delicate and could break. "Talk to me. What's going on?"

She shook her head again, harder, feeling the slipknot brushing against the nape of her neck. "I can't. Seriously, let's just get out of here."

He sighed. "Fine. But first . . ." He clasped both of her hands in his.

She tried to tug away. *Just friends,* that's what they'd said. That's what they both wanted—or, at least, all they could handle. But he held tight.

"You look, uh, really pretty," he said.

She looked down. He was stepping on the lily. "Thanks," she murmured.

He crossed over to her side and put an arm around her waist, just like he always had in the old days. The crushed lily no longer looked like a flower. It was just a broken heap of white ground into the cement.

"Come on, Cinderella," Adam said gently. "Let's go to the ball."

Stop giggling, Miranda Stevens told herself.

But she couldn't help it.

"Looks like you got something on your dress," Kane said, rubbing his fingers against the soft green silk. "I think it's just water."

She giggled.

"What?"

"Nothing." She giggled again. No surprise: It's what girls did around the great Kane Geary. Miranda had always prided herself on being different, but now she understood. She had to giggle. Not because it was cute, or because she was trying to be more feminine. But because it was ridiculous.

Kane Geary, in a tuxedo, his arm stiff around her waist, posing for the camera.

Kane Geary, prom date.

Kane Geary . . . boyfriend.

You just had to laugh. Or, in Miranda's case, giggle.

"Miranda, what's up with you tonight?" Kane asked. He had started calling her Miranda after Vegas, after the kiss. Before, it had always been "Stevens." But now, things were different.

"Nothing. Really." She rolled her eyes at her mother and slid her finger across her throat, the message clear: *Picture time is over.* And, uncharacteristically, her mother obeyed, hurrying across the expansive backyard to gossip with Harper's parents. Mrs. Grace was brimming with tears over the way her "little girl" was all grown up. Miranda's mother, on the other hand, was just relieved, and—as she never tired of pointing out—shocked that Miranda had scored a date.

Kane turned her around in his arms so they were facing each other, then leaned down and kissed her. He tasted like spearmint and gin. "Have I told you how beautiful you look tonight?"

No need to suck up, she was about to joke. *I already agreed to go with you.*

But she cut herself off. She wasn't his buddy anymore, she was his *girlfriend*—but she wouldn't be for long if she couldn't figure out how to act the part.

"Thank you," she cooed. "And you look really handsome."

He gave her a strange look, then smiled. It wasn't the famous Kane smirk, crooked and mysterious and all-knowing; it was just an ordinary smile. Then his hand was warm against her neck, softly kneading the tight muscles, and she closed her eyes. "And what have I done to deserve this?" she asked, sighing blissfully.

"Nothing," he whispered in her ear, pausing to quickly kiss the lobe. "You can owe me one."

She glanced at him, expecting to see mischief in his face, some deliciously devious anticipation of the IOU, but nothing was there but the placid smile. She smiled back, and then there was silence.

All those years, all that banter . . . and suddenly, they had nothing left to say.

"Maybe, um, we should go check on Harper?" she suggested, tipping her head toward the edge of the backyard where Harper was chatting animatedly with her date and obviously doing a fine job of taking care of herself.

"Good idea." Kane grabbed her hand and led her across the yard as she tried to keep her sharp heels from digging too deeply into the Graces' finely manicured lawn.

They caught Harper with her head thrown back in authentic-sounding laughter. Only a best friend could have known it was utterly fake. "Jake was just telling me about the time he got drunk off his ass and ended up streaking naked through a PTA meeting," Harper said, gasping for breath. She gave Kane a sharp poke on the shoulder. "Is there a reason you waited so long to introduce me to your only nonloser friend?"

Kane raised an eyebrow. "I like him too much to punish him like that, Grace."

"Very funny." Harper pulled back her lips in a gruesomely exaggerated smile. "So why now?"

Kane shrugged. "What can I tell you? He lost a bet."

Everyone laughed, except for Jake—a dark-haired senior from the next town over who was built like a quarterback and grinned like a talk-show host. "*He* is going to the prom with the hottest girl in town," he said, wrapping an arm around Harper's shoulders. She slipped out of his grip.

"Hotness takes work, boys," she said, grabbing Miranda's wrist. "So *we* are off to make ourselves beautiful, and then"—she shot a look over her shoulder at the horde of eager parents—"we can get the hell out of here and have some real fun." Harper dragged Miranda into the kitchen and shut the sliding-glass door behind them. "Kill me now."

"That bad?"

Harper wandered into the living room and threw herself down on one of the couches. "He's fine. Whatever. I told you this was a bad idea. I didn't want to go."

Miranda snorted. "Like I was really going to let you sulk in your room on prom night. You think I could have any fun knowing you were lying in bed crying about—"

She fell silent under Harper's steely glare.

"I'm over him," Harper said steadily.

"Right. I know." So over Adam that she hid every time she saw him coming down the hall. So over him that every time Miranda—unwisely—said his name, Harper's face flushed red, then turned to stone. "You're totally over him. Which is why we thought—"

"*We*," Harper cackled. "I love it. Kane Geary has never been a *we* in his life—I still don't get how you did it."

Miranda flopped down on the couch next to her. "Yeah, I'm a regular superhero."

"The power to leap tall buildings and melt the hearts of ice-cold bastards."

"Just call me Wonder Woman," Miranda said sourly. "As in, I wonder what the hell I'm doing."

"Trouble in paradise?"

"We're talking about *you*," Miranda pointed out. "Jake is perfectly nice—and, in case you didn't notice, hot. I wouldn't let Kane set you up with a loser."

"He's not a loser," Harper admitted. "He's just not . . ."

Not Adam.

The Eiffel Tower–shaped poster board was peeling off the wall, the sparkling lights dangling from the ceiling had mostly burned out, and the faux champagne tasted like sugar water. So much for Midnight in Paris.

"Isn't it the coolest?" Emma Logan asked, grinning idiotically at her fellow prom princesses, assembled in a neat row of chairs across the stage. "It's like we're really in Paris." She pointed at the river of blue balloons that wound its way around the edge of the gymnasium. "Look, it's like the Thames!"

Harper rubbed her forehead, careful not to accidentally smudge her mascara. "First of all, it's not *Thames*—" She pronounced it as Emma had, rhyming with "James." "And, second of all, that's in London." *Idiot,* she wanted to add, but even though she no longer cared about these girls, or their A-list boyfriends, or the masses of hangers-on who followed all of them around like lost kittens, some reflex forced her to finish the sentence with a graceful, self-deprecating smile, as if apologizing for not being just as dumb.

"God, did you, like, sleep through geography class?" Sara Walker piped up from Harper's other side. "It's totally supposed to be the Seine." She pronounced it "seen." This time, Harper didn't bother to correct her. Nor did she point out that Sara's dress looked more like a potato sack than a prom gown. Except for the color—*that* just looked like cat puke.

The vice principal took the stage, pulling his tuxedo jacket down over his lumpy potbelly. Harper could see the sweat running down the back of his neck. "Welcome to the Haven High Senior Prom!" he shouted into the mic, and, possibly for the first time in his career, he was rewarded with a round of sincere and thundering applause. "Are you all having a good time?"

More cheering. Harper clapped too, bringing her hands together so sharply, her palms stung. The pain helped wake her up.

"Behind me, you see some of the loveliest ladies in all the land," the vice principal said, holding out his hands to stem the drunken wolf whistles. "And tonight, one lucky princess is going to become a queen." A mousy sophomore scurried onstage and handed the vice principal a tiara. From where Harper was sitting, it looked like a jewel-encrusted crown, sparkling in the light like a lattice of diamonds. But she knew better. It was mostly cardboard, paste, and sequins, with a few rhinestones stuck on for good measure.

The sophomore handed him a small white envelope and then, with a wide-eyed glance at the prom court—a look that said, *just maybe, someday, don't laugh, but it could be me*—rushed off the stage. Emma was grabbing handfuls of her dress and twisting them into tight knots while Sara gripped the edges of her chair, her bloodless fingers turning white. Then the vice principal opened the envelope, and every girl onstage sucked in a sharp, terrified breath.

Every girl except Harper, who—unlike the rest of them—hadn't campaigned, hadn't tallied a crowd of friends and admirers who'd promised to vote for her, wasn't darting glances at the competition and trying to convince herself that her smile was brighter, her hair shinier, her breasts perkier, her chances better.

Partly because she just didn't care anymore, or at least she didn't want to.

Partly because she knew who she was, and what she deserved. And so did everyone else.

"So without further ado, your new prom queen is . . . Harper Grace!"

There was a flurry of squealing, and Emma and Sara gave her a hug. They all hated her.

Harper stood up, crossed the stage, and accepted her crown. It looked fake and cheap close up. The metal dug into the skin at her temples. If she kept it on all night, she was going to get a headache.

Harper raised her hand and gave the crowd her best Miss America wave. The warm roar of appreciation that greeted her was almost enough to puncture the numbness—almost, but not quite.

"On to prom king," the vice principal continued, placing a meaty hand on Harper's shoulder. She forced herself not to shrug it off. "Let's see who will be lucky enough to get the spotlight dance with our queen."

And *now* Harper felt her stomach clench. She wiped her palms against her dress and tried not to show that she cared. She *didn't* care, she told herself. Whoever was elected king, that's who she would dance with.

And if it was him, then so be it. She would dance with him, just as she'd done plenty of times before. And she would feel nothing. Because she was over him. Because he had chosen Beth; he had proven that Harper meant nothing to him, or at least didn't mean enough, which was just as bad. She would stand across from him and lace her arms around his shoulders. She would inhale his cologne, that deep, musky scent that smelled like the center of a forest. She would lean in, feel his breath on her cheek, press her chin into his shoulder, and sway. She would let him hold her, let his hands rest warm and solid at her hips, let his body press against hers—only because she had to. Because it was an obligation, the responsibility of winners.

She would do what she was supposed to do, and she would feel nothing. Because she was over him. So she didn't care if he lost—and didn't care if he won.

"And your new prom king . . . Adam Morgan! Come up onstage, Adam, to collect your crown and your queen!" The applause faded away, and the crowd drifted to the edges of the dance floor as a cheesy love song came through the speakers.

> *You're mine, all of the time.*
> *I belong in your eyes . . .*

A spotlight lit the empty floor. And Adam still hadn't appeared. Someone laughed.

"Adam Morgan," the vice principal said again. His hand, still on Harper's shoulder, was beginning to sweat. "Has anyone seen Adam Morgan?"

"Kid's not here!" someone shouted from the crowd.

"King me!" someone else called out. "I got what she needs!"

Harper scoured their faces, looking for his. The music played on.

With you I live,
Without you I cry,
Without you I die . . .

This is pathetic, Harper thought. So stupid. So high school. So beneath her. But the spotlight shined, the music played, and the floor was empty.

Her body on autopilot, Harper walked to the edge of the stage and descended the stairs, keeping her head up and her shoulders back. She crossed the floor, the crowd opening up to let her pass, and found herself in the middle of the dance floor, alone.

She wouldn't cry. That wasn't her style. But inside, where no one could see . . . inside, it felt like something was on fire.

And then strong arms were around her waist, holding her steady, and she was swaying with the music, and, for a moment, everything was as it should be.

But it wasn't Adam.

"Congratulations, Your Highness," the boy whispered in her ear. It took her a moment to come back to herself, to remember. Not Adam. It was her date, come to rescue her.

The boy—Jake, she remembered—held tight. "It was no contest," he murmured. "Compared to you, the rest of these girls are total dogs."

She knew she should say thank you. But she didn't want to speak. She didn't want to be there at all. She wanted to disappear; she wanted *him* to disappear.

He tugged her tighter and pressed his cheek against the top of her head. He smelled wrong. Like coffee and deodorant. Harper pulled back and looked at his face, really *looked* at it, for the first time that night. It was ruddy and well proportioned, with all the right features in all the right places. His eyes were brown and sparkly, his nose slightly too large; he had a dimple in his left cheek and a cleft in his chin. "Thanks for bringing me tonight," he said, his breath slightly sour from Kane's bootleg gin.

He waited for an answer. Instead, she kissed him.

With you I live,
Without you I die . . .

The numbness descended again, saving her. He rubbed his hands up and down her back, like Adam, but not Adam. She closed her eyes, but there was no fooling herself, no pretending that he was anything but a stranger. No pretending he was anyone else. His fingers cold against her skin, he brushed her hair back, and kissed her, and kissed her, and the song refused to end and he refused to let go.

And it was as she had imagined it.

She felt nothing.

chapter

2

"Shut the hell up!" Reed shouted, throwing his empty bottle against the wall. It smashed to pieces, the glass spraying through the air and clattering against the linoleum. "Just shut up." He leaned forward until his face was nearly pressed into the beat-up couch that smelled like mildew, and tucked his head between his arms, trying to drown out the noise.

To drown out everything.

"Dude, what's your deal?" Fish asked, appearing in the doorway. He was still holding his drumsticks.

"Just give it up," Reed said. He took another swig of the tequila. His head throbbed. Why was even he still awake? The liquor and pot were supposed to knock him out, or at least make things blurry and painless. But his eyes were open, and his mind was too clear.

It was the rage. Nothing had been able to stop it, not for weeks. Not the drinking, not the smoking, not the pills. He was too angry, and whatever he did to try to avoid it only backfired. The drinking fueled the rage. The pot trapped his mind in an endless loop—Beth. Kaia. Beth in his arms. Kaia in the car, broken. Smashed. Beth's lips. Kaia's smile. Death.

And now he had a new image to play with: Beth and Adam.

It was his own fault. He didn't know what he'd been thinking, dressing up like a penguin, crawling back there like nothing had happened, like he could give her a second chance after everything she'd done, like they could start fresh. Maybe he'd imagined that she was hurting too, that he wasn't the only one who lay around all day choking on fumes and cursing everything. It had been a mistake. Just the latest in a long line.

"We're rehearsing, man," Hale complained, unstrapping his guitar. "*Your* idea, before you flaked."

"I'm back now, aren't I?"

Fish threw a drumstick at him. "Yeah, you're back, drunk and stoned, and you didn't even bring any of the good stuff to share. So what good are you?"

"You wanna rehearse?" Reed pushed himself off the couch, then staggered as the world tipped beneath him. He collapsed backward, his head slamming against the wall with a dull thud and a sharp pain. "Let's rehearse."

Hale snorted. "You're worthless like this. Get some sleep."

"Is this a joke?" Reed sneered. "*You're* calling *me* a slacker?" He was the one who always wanted to rehearse. He was the one who booked them gigs, who wrote the songs, who wanted them to go on tour—or, at least, he had been.

These days, there didn't seem to be much point.

He grabbed for a half-open beer, missed, and sent it flying across the room. "Shit! Thassa last one."

"You're a mess, kid," Fish said.

Reed peered up at him, at his stringy blond hair, sallow face, bloodshot eyes, ready to argue. A mess? If anyone was a mess, it was . . .

But he lost the thought. Just like he'd lost everything else.

"I'm sorry," Beth said again. "Really, I'm so sorry."

Adam squeezed her hand. "Stop. It's okay."

Beth leaned back on her swing and tipped her head up to the sky. "It's not okay." She shivered and rubbed her hands along her bare arms.

"Cold?"

She shook her head, but Adam draped his tuxedo jacket around her shoulders. Instead of sitting back down on his swing, he stayed behind her and gave her a gentle push. Her heels skidded across the dirt.

"You can go now, if you want," she told him. "I'm okay. Really."

"And I'm okay here, too."

She didn't try to convince him, even though she almost believed it was true, that if he left, she would be okay—at least as long as she stayed on the playground. These days, it was the only place where she felt safe, the only place where she could quiet all the accusing voices in her mind. Tonight, it had seemed like the only place to hide.

"I can't believe I made you miss your senior prom," she told him. "I suck."

Adam grabbed her shoulders and pulled the swing to a stop. "Don't say that." His voice was low and steady. Insistent.

She scared him, she knew that. After what had happened in Las Vegas—after standing on a ledge, waiting to take that last step, discovering how much she wanted to—she scared herself. It was why she didn't want to be alone.

"Prom's not over yet," she said. "You could still make it, and maybe she—" Beth cut herself off. It was their unspoken agreement. She never talked about Reed. He never talked about Harper.

And neither of them talked about Kaia.

Adam let go of her. He sat down on his swing again and pushed himself off, into the air, back and forth, his body awkwardly large and long, his legs pumping, his mouth open in a silent howl to the wind.

"Why are you being so nice to me?" she asked, mostly because she didn't think he would hear.

But he did. "I just want to."

"After what I did?"

He stopped swinging and turned toward her. "Beth, it's *over*," he said firmly. "You have to let it go. Start over."

She nodded. He made it sound so easy.

Adam suddenly stood up. "Let's dance," he said.

"What?"

He grinned, and in the dark she could still catch a glimmer of the little-kid enthusiasm she'd fallen for years ago. "It's prom, right? Let's dance."

"It's not prom. You're *missing* the prom—to babysit me." Because when Reed had left her house she had burst into tears, even though she had forbidden herself to fall apart all over again. And even though she had forbidden herself to let Adam pick up the pieces, *again*, she had let him hug her, and hold her, and take her somewhere safe.

"So you owe me," Adam pointed out. He reached for her hand and pulled her off the swing.

The bottom of her gown was covered in dirt she'd kicked up on the swing. It didn't matter; she'd never wear the dress again. "There's no music."

Adam laughed. "No way am I singing. Just use your imagination."

She let him grab her by the waist, and then she put her arms around his shoulders and they swayed, listening to the crickets and the rustling breeze. Beth closed her eyes, and again, she asked a question so softly that she assumed—she hoped—he wouldn't hear.

"Do you love her?"

And this time, he didn't hear.

Or at least, he didn't answer.

The official Haven High PTA post-prom extravaganza had it all: a rock-climbing wall, a row of slot machines, a go-cart track, semi-edible snacks from every restaurant in town—and a horde of gorgeous, glamorous, inebriated girls with low-cut dresses and high-octane libidos.

And Kane wasn't allowed to touch any of them.

He wasn't even allowed to look.

"What did you say?" With painful effort, he tore himself away from the forbidden fruit and turned back to his date. His *girlfriend*, he thought, surprised as always that the word didn't incite a shudder or anaphylactic shock. There was instead just a general wave of unsteadiness, like the way he always felt the day before getting sick or the day after getting smashed.

"I said, do you want to go with them?" Miranda asked, nodding toward the guys who were cutting out early, headed for a post-post prom party in the desert. Although, knowing these guys, "party" meant "getting stoned, getting stupid, having lots of sex" and then repeating the cycle until dawn broke. Just what the doctor ordered to wash away the sickeningly sweet taste of prom.

"No," Kane said quickly, taking Miranda's hand. That's what couples did, right? "Unless you want to, Miranda."

"It could be fun," she said.

For Miranda? About as fun as getting a pencil jammed in her eye, and she knew it.

"I'd rather just stay here," he lied. "We haven't gotten to try out the rock-climbing wall yet. It, uh, looks like fun."

It looked like loser central. But at least he was trying.

God, was he trying.

She rolled her eyes. "Can I talk to you for a second?"

"Whatever you want," he said. "It's your special night." Now he was making *himself* nauseated. And all he got for his trouble was another eye-roll.

Their hands clasped, she led him through the crowd of seniors stuffing their face, around the slot machines, and out the back door. The PTA mother stationed there informed them that, once they left, they wouldn't be allowed in. Miranda grimaced. "I think we'll live."

Kane drew in a deep breath. The air inside had tasted like cotton candy and hairspray. It was the taste of feeble love poetry and awkward slow-dancing and virgins hoping against hope to get laid. He'd almost suffocated.

Miranda looked up at him, then down, then up again, then seemed to come to some kind of decision. "What's the deal, Kane?" she asked. "Why are you being like this?"

"What are you talking about, Miranda?"

"I'm talking about *that*," she snapped. "*Miranda?* Since when do you call me Miranda?"

"Okay, *Stevens*," he retorted. "If you want to talk about out of character, since when do you want to hit some skeezy stoner after party? Since when do you giggle?"

"I do *not* giggle."

Kane raised his voice to a flighty falsetto. "Oh, Kane, let's dance. I just *love* this song. Giggle giggle. Oh, Kane, you're so funny! Giggle giggle. Oh, Kane—"

"Shut up."

"All night long, Stevens. And it's been going on for *weeks*."

"And how about you?" she argued. "Buttering me up like we're on a reality-TV show and you're lobbying for a rose?" She put on a false baritone. "Why, Miranda, you look so pretty in that dress. Miranda, have you always been so beautiful? Miranda, why would I ever want to look at any other girls when I'm with the most wonderful one there is?"

"I would *never* talk like that," he said indignantly.

"Oh, really? So you were looking at other girls in there?"

"Of course not! Why would I want to when—" He slammed his lips together and glared at her. Point taken. "What do you want from me?" he finally asked. "I'm just trying to be a good boyfriend."

"And I'm just trying to be a good girlfriend!"

They were both silent for a moment. And then they burst into laughter.

"We're doing a pretty crap-ass job of it, aren't we, Stevens?"

"At least I have an excuse," she pointed out. "This is new for me. But you? If you got a dollar for every girl you've been with, you'd be a millionaire . . . and, uh, technically a male prostitute. But you get my point."

"Hey!"

She flinched. "I'm sorry—did I offend you? I didn't mean—"

"Hell yes, you offended me. Thank god." He smirked at her. "Bring it on." He grabbed her hands and pulled her close to him, loving the way her tiny body fit in his arms. "You're not some simpering bimbo," he reminded her. "You're sarcastic and obnoxious and overcritical—"

"And you're a shallow, insensitive, egomaniacal, self-centered asshole," she countered, grazing her hand across his cheek.

"And you can't resist me," he said smugly.

She grinned defiantly at him. "Sweet-talk me all you want, I'm still not sleeping with you."

"Who said anything about sex?"

"You didn't have to say anything." She raised her eyebrows. "I know you, sex maniac. And I know that you're the one who can't resist *me*."

He laughed. "Forget what I just said. Where's the sweet, subservient, giggly Miranda? Let's get her back here. This one's kind of annoying."

"She went to bed. Guess you're stuck with me." She rose up on her toes.

"Punishment for all my sins." He kissed her.

This is Miranda, he reminded himself, as he often did when he looked down to discover her wrapped in his arms. He still couldn't believe it, and he wasn't sure what was stranger: That now, whenever he saw Miranda, short, loudmouthed, neurotic *Miranda*, all he wanted to do was run his fingers across her skin, brush her red hair away from her sparkling green eyes, and taste-test her lips to see whether she'd opted for strawberry or peach lip gloss that morning. Or, maybe stranger yet, that he'd never noticed any of it before.

Kane was an expert in many things, but girls were at the top of the list. No detail escaped his notice, no cleavage, no ass, no freckled cheek or husky laugh flew too low for his radar. But until last month, Miranda had hidden in plain sight. The brainy one, the perpetual sidekick, the girl with a million complaints, twice as many insecurities, and a permanent membership in the "just one of the boys" club. Or so he'd always thought.

Kane hated to be wrong—but, better late than never, he was now thoroughly enjoying being right.

Her lips were firm and warm, and he rubbed his hands across her back, slipping his fingers beneath the edge of the green satin to massage her smooth skin. He could feel her smiling through the kiss as she ran her fingers through his hair and then rested her hands at the nape of his neck, kneading his muscles, clinging to him.

Miranda Stevens, he thought again, opening his eyes to take in her pale eyelids and the long, reddish lashes that brushed her cheeks. *Unbelievable.*

They finally broke for air, their foreheads still pressed

together. Her face was flushed. "We'll figure this out," she whispered. "Right?"

"We'll get it eventually," he said. "We're very smart."

"I am, at least."

"Watch it, Stevens." He grabbed her waist and lifted her off her feet. "Remember, I'm bigger than you."

She reached out and tickled the spot on his neck just above his left collarbone, and he convulsed with laughter, dropping her back to the ground. It was his only weak spot; most people didn't know it existed.

"So . . . now that we're being honest and all that . . ." Her flushed face turned an even deeper pink. "Can I ask a question?"

He gave her a he-man pose. "Yes, I am a male model. Why do you ask?"

She smacked his chest lightly. "Seriously."

"Okay. Seriously."

"Are you . . . sorry? You know. About us?"

Kane couldn't help thinking about the girls still inside the party. Many were, as he knew from personal experience, better kissers. Many were better looking, better dressed. But none were actually better.

"No regrets, Stevens." He kissed her again. There was so much he had to lie to her about—it felt surprisingly good, for once, to tell the truth.

Adam froze midway up the walk. She was sitting on his front stoop, the silver dress sparkling under the porch light, her thick, wavy hair doing its best to escape from an elaborate upsweep. Her heels lay at the bottom of the steps; her toes were painted red.

"Hey." Harper smiled sadly as he approached. It was the first time she'd spoken to him since that night in Vegas.

"Hey."

"Nice tux." She leaned backward, her bare back pressed against the porch steps. "My dress matches your boutonniere." She laughed, once. "Funny."

He sat down next to her, aware of how close their hands were, aware of the space between them. "What are you doing here, Gracie?" he asked softly.

"Congratulations." She reached behind her and handed him a cardboard crown, painted gold and covered in fake jewels. "Prom king."

He laid the crown on the stoop, picturing the night he'd missed, and a terrible thought occurred to him. "And prom queen . . ."

She nodded. "As if there was ever any doubt." There was a shadow of the old Harper haughtiness in that last part, but only a trace, so insubstantial that he wasn't sure it had been there at all.

"Congratulations." The prom king and queen always shared a spotlight dance. If he had been there . . . but he hadn't.

Harper bared her teeth, though it wasn't quite a smile. "Yes, it's a true honor," she said. "I've got everything I want in the world." And again, there was a slight trace of a familiar bitterness, but then it was gone, and she just looked sad.

"Why are you here?" he said again.

Harper looked down, playing with the strap on her small silver bag. "I know she's your ex," she said quietly. "And I know you still care about her, even after—" She swallowed hard. "What she did. You may not believe me, but I even know she's not the only one to blame. I'm not saying she should go to jail. I'm not even saying she should be miserable for the rest of her life. *I* was the one up on that roof with her, Adam. I was the one who—"

"I know, and—"

"Adam, I need you to not talk for a minute, okay?" There was no emotion in her voice. "Just let me say this. Can you do that?"

He nodded.

"I was up on that roof, and I meant what I said to her, and if someone wants to be her friend, fine. Great. Kaia's dead. I can't fix that. And no matter what happens, even if . . ." She drew in a sharp breath. "I can't fix it. She can't fix it. So she gets to move on with her life. Fine. But why you? That's what I don't get, Ad. Why does it have to be you?"

There was a pause, and she looked at him expectantly.

"Now I talk?" he asked.

She nodded.

"She needs me," he said simply. "There's no one else."

Harper rubbed the back of her hand against her eyes, like a little kid. "What if I needed you? What if I told you that I couldn't survive without you, that I was weak and lonely and you're the only person who can make things okay?"

"Is that true?"

Her eyes widened, like she wished it could be. But then she shook her head. "I don't need you. I want you. And you . . . I know you do. I can *see* that you do."

He grabbed her hands and pressed them to his lips.

"I want you," she whispered. "You're *my* best friend, you're *mine*, and I want you back."

"That was your call, not mine," he said. "Say the word, and I'm back."

Harper drew her hands away. "She put something in my drink," she said, too calmly. "She put something in my drink, and I got in a car, and Kaia died. And if that doesn't matter to you—"

"Of course it matters!"

"She should be in jail," Harper said flatly.

He tensed. "You promised you wouldn't say anything—"

"Don't." There was ice in her voice. "Don't defend her to me. Don't try to protect her from me. Just don't."

"Harper, I know you're mad, but if you tell . . ."

"Shut up!" She smashed her hand against the stoop. "I'm not telling anyone," she said more quietly. "If she goes down, I go down. I was . . . I was the one behind the wheel."

He reached out a hand, touched her shoulder, but she pushed him away. "I'm not *her*," she snapped. "I don't need your pity. I don't *need* anything."

And that was the problem. Harper was strong. Harper *didn't* need him—not the way Beth did. Adam couldn't just walk away from that. Much as he may have wanted to.

It couldn't matter what he wanted. Not after—he shut his eyes, seeing it again, as he did almost every day, the image of her blond hair rising over the ledge, climbing back to solid ground. She'd come so close. . . .

He couldn't let it happen again.

"You can't have us both, Adam. You get that, right? After what she did to Kaia, to me . . . you don't get to be okay with that. Not if you want—" She shook her head. "It doesn't matter. I just need you to say it. That's why I came here, I guess. I need you to look at me and say it. You pick her."

"I'm not picking *anyone*," Adam protested.

"Yeah. You're not." She nodded, but didn't raise her head again. She sat slumped, her chin pressed to her chest a moment, and then looked up, her eyes dry. "So I guess we're done."

"Harper, I wish . . ."

"Just do me a favor and forget we had this little chat, okay?" she asked. "It's humiliating."

"It's not," he said. "I'm glad you came." It sounded so lame. Formal, like he was bidding farewell to a party guest.

"You should probably go inside now." She was covering her mouth with her hands, which muffled her voice. "I'm just going to sit here for a while."

He stood up. "Okay." She didn't watch him walk up the steps and toward the house. She just kept staring out at the street. He paused in the doorway. "Gracie?"

She didn't say anything.

"You look—" He wanted to tell her how beautiful she looked. But he'd already told Beth the same thing. Somehow, it felt like Harper would know. And that would make things worse. "Get home safe, okay?"

"Good night, Adam."

He went inside and, for a long time, watched her through the peephole. But she never turned around, so he never saw her face. She stayed perfectly still. He went upstairs, took off the tuxedo, brushed his teeth, washed his face, and when he came back down, she was still there. He finally went to bed, knowing she might stay for hours.

And knowing that, by morning, she would be gone.

chapter

3

"Who doesn't buy a *yearbook*?" Miranda asked, pulling hers out of her locker and running her hand across the rich leather binding. "What's wrong with you?"

"A hundred bucks for a picture book filled with people you hate?" Kane argued. "What's wrong with *you*?"

"We survived high school," Miranda said. "We should get to enjoy the rewards."

"There's only one reward," Kane said. "Getting the hell out."

She smacked the yearbook against his chest. "Do you want it now, or what?"

"What for?"

"So you can sign it, jerk. Write me a loving message about everything I mean to you."

Kane leaned toward her and nuzzled his face into her neck. Miranda flushed with pleasure. She'd never expected to be half of one of those PDA couples, but now she couldn't get enough of those DAs, public or not. "How about I save us both some time," Kane murmured, guiding her behind a bank of lockers, "and just tell you right now how much I—"

"Yo, Geary!"

They broke apart as a handful of Kane's ex-teammates loped down the hall. "Dude, awesome yearbook photo," one of them said, flipping his book open and pointing to the photo of an extended middle finger sitting over Kane's name. "Which of those yearbook chicks did you have to screw to pull that off?"

"Hope it wasn't the butt-ugly one," another said, laughing. "Because it wasn't *that* awesome."

"I have my ways, gentlemen," Kane said smoothly. Miranda edged away from him. He didn't stop her.

"Sorry, shorty," the first guy said, leering at Miranda. "Didn't see you down there." He noticed the yearbook in her hand. "*You're* a senior? I thought you were like, a fresh-man or something."

Miranda had been going to school with him for seven years, and had spent junior year health class staring at the back of his oversize head. Apparently, she hadn't made much of an impression.

"Kane, I've gotta go," she said quietly. "I'm late for class, and I've got this test—"

Kane ruffled her hair—he never remembered how much she hated that. It made her feel like a little kid, which was a feeling that, at five feet tall, she got plenty of. "Stevens here is a total brainiac," he bragged.

Miranda blushed. "Kane . . ."

"Not so smart to hook up with this guy," the other jock said, clapping Kane on the back and laughing. "Now, if you ever want to get with a *real* man . . ."

"Knock it off, O'Hara," Kane said, wrapping an arm around Miranda and tugging her toward him. "She belongs to me."

It was all so caveman. "I don't *belong* to anyone," Miranda snapped, stepping away.

The jocks laughed. "Watch out, Geary. She's tough. Don't let her whip you."

Kane leered. "Not to kiss and tell, gentlemen, but if anyone here's getting whipped—"

"I'm out of here," Miranda said loudly.

He shrugged, barely even glancing in her direction. "Cool. Later, Stevens."

Miranda glared at him. "Yeah. Later." And she stormed down the hall, seething.

He caught up with her just before she stepped into her classroom. She ignored him, but he grabbed the strap of her bag and tugged her back.

"I have a test," she said.

"You're mad."

Miranda glared. "Now who's the brainiac?"

"Why are you being so uptight?"

"Why are you being such a jerk?"

Kane sighed. "I thought we agreed we were going to be ourselves. I was just having a little fun—isn't that what we're supposed to be doing?" He tugged on her ponytail. "You know, I hear that when a guy teases you, usually it's just because he likes you."

She couldn't hold back the smile. "Your friends are idiots."

"No argument here."

"I've got a test," Miranda said. "I'm going inside."

"Hey." He stopped her again and held out his hand. "What about your yearbook?"

It was impossible to stay mad at him. "Write something nice," she warned, handing him the book.

"I'm always nice," he said, wiggling his eyebrows. He leaned toward her. "There's something I forgot to tell you about your test."

"What?"

He kissed her.

And that afternoon, when he finally gave the yearbook back to her, she thought about the kiss, about how sweet it had been, how soft and kind and tender, no matter how he was acting. When she read his yearbook entry, her heart plunging in disappointment, even as she berated herself for having stupid expectations—she thought about the kiss.

> *Stevens,*
> *Who knew that mouth could do more than argue?*
> *You're a true-blue friend, a red-hot lady, and all that*
> *other good yearbook shit. You've got a big heart, and*
> *I've got an even* bigger *. . . you know. So we're*
> *both winners.*
>
> *KG*

It didn't mean anything, she told herself. Guys didn't talk about their feelings, didn't write them in yearbooks, no matter what she'd been hoping. It didn't mean they didn't feel anything at all. She didn't need him to say it. She didn't need him to write it.

Not when she had his kiss—that said it all.

Adam balled up the pale blue slip and threw it halfway across the room, right into the trash can. Three points.

A blue pass was never a good sign.

The study hall teacher gave him a sympathetic look, then waved him out the door. And he began the long, slow march to the guidance office, running through the past several weeks in his head, searching for what he'd done wrong. The last time he'd sat in Ms. Campbell's cramped, cluttered office, facing down her Ben Franklin glasses (with hairstyle to match), she had given him a shape-up-or-ship out lecture that culminated in the only persuasive threat in the guidance counselor arsenal: Get your grades up and your shit together, or you won't graduate.

Not in those words, of course.

Hating her, hating school and, most days, hating his life, Adam had still followed orders. Now his grades—reliably mediocre—were, in fact, the only thing he could count on. He opened the door to her office, steeling himself against the cloying taffy scent—with an undercurrent of cigarettes—that always made him choke. Then he put on his best golden-boy smile, ready to convince the counselor that Haven High's record-breaking, all-American pride and joy was back in business.

He needn't have bothered.

"Coach?" he said in confusion.

Coach Wilson was sitting behind the desk, his large frame penned in by the menagerie of windup figures and china figurines that blanketed the surface. "They're doing some construction over in the athletic wing—your counselor said we could use her office for our meeting." The coach stood up. "This is him, our star."

The man sitting across from Coach Wilson stood up and grasped Adam's hand, pumping it up and down. "A pleasure," he said. "The coach was showing me some game tapes, and that shot you got off in the play-offs? *Nice.*"

"Uh . . . thanks," Adam said, shooting a helpless look at his coach.

"And your foul-shot ratio is damn impressive," the guy continued, "though we may have to work on your shooting stance—it's a little loose, but that's easily fixed with the proper training. No offense, Coach," he said, turning toward Coach Wilson, who'd settled back into the guidance counselor's chair.

"Hey, you're the expert," the coach said, grinning. "I'm just a lil' old high school coach. What do I know?"

"Enough to beat me eleven-three last time we played," the guy pointed out.

"Oh, that's right!" The coach slapped his forehead in exaggerated surprise. "I forgot all about that."

"Bullshit. It's all I heard about for a month."

"Uh, Coach?" Adam nodded toward the clock. "My next class is going to start soon, and—"

"Where are my manners?" the guy said, indicating that Adam should take a seat. "The name's Brian Foley. Your coach and I went to high school together, back in the stone age."

"Brian's a coach now at UC-Riverside," his coach said, giving Adam a meaningful look.

"Here's the deal, Adam," the UC guy said. "I've got a last-minute spot on next year's squad, and I want you." He tossed Adam a white-and-yellow T-shirt reading UCR HIGH-LANDERS. "You've got Highlander written all over you."

"Me? But—I didn't even apply to Riverside," Adam said. "I'm going to State, in Borrega."

The UC coach snorted. "Do they even have a basket-ball team? Listen to what I'm telling you, Adam. I *want* you on my team. And I can *get* you on my team. Doesn't matter if you applied to the school or not. I've seen your transcripts, I can get you admitted. I may even be able to manage a scholarship. It'll take some doing, but . . . I've seen you play, and you're the guy to play for me."

"You can really do all that?" Adam asked, trying to process. He was going to the state school in Borrega, that had always been the plan. It was an hour away from home, one step up from community college, and everyone he knew would be there too. Harper would be there.

"Adam, my friend, welcome to the wonderful world of college athletics." Coach Foley stretched back in his seat. "I can do pretty much anything I want. And, once you're a Highlander, so can you."

Adam squirmed under the guy's fiercely confident stare. "I don't know . . ." He'd been counting the days until he could finally get out of school and never come back. Moving hundreds of miles away to some strange place where he wouldn't know anyone, and would need to work even harder than he had in high school? What was the point? "School's not really my thing."

"Morgan, be smart," Coach Wilson said. "This is your shot. It's what we in the coaching biz like to call a win–win situation. Don't pass it up."

"He doesn't have to decide right now," the UC coach

said, standing up. He leaned over and shook Adam's hand again. "You've got two weeks." He handed Adam a business card. Adam stared down at it, stunned, still expecting the whole thing to be a joke. But the card looked real. And both coaches looked dead serious. "Call me by June fourteenth, if you're interested. Otherwise the spot goes to someone else." He waved good-bye to Coach Wilson and headed for the door, pausing to give Adam one last once-over. "Your coach here is a wise man," he said. "And he's given you some good advice. Be smart, like he says. You're on the foul line now, kid, and you only get one shot."

"I'm really going to miss you," Ms. Polansky said, signing Beth's yearbook with a flourish. Her picture was next to a large empty spot, where Mr. Powell's photo had been yanked days before the yearbook went to press, leaving the staff no time to redesign the page. When they'd set their production schedule, they hadn't factored in the possibility that Haven's newest teacher was living under a false name, on the run from a teen sex scandal.

Beth could have given them a clue. Even now, she could still remember the sour taste of Powell's mouth and feel his fingers digging into her shoulders as he struggled to hold her in place. But she'd kept her mouth shut. Just another mistake.

"I'll miss you, too," Beth told her junior year English teacher, wishing she could slip back in time. Things had been easy when she was a junior; *life* had been easy.

"Oh, I doubt it," the teacher said, laughing. The rare smile made her look several years younger. Although Beth knew that Ms. Polansky had been intimidating Haven

High students ever since her parents were in school, she sometimes had trouble believing that the lithe, impeccably tailored woman in front of her was well into her sixties. "Once you get to Berkeley, you'll forget all about us—you'll get a chance to see what *real* teaching is like."

Beth flushed and dipped her head, letting her blond hair fall over her eyes. "I, um, didn't get into Berkeley," she admitted to the woman who'd written her a rave recommendation for her dream school.

Ms. Polansky pursed her lips, then gave a sharp nod. "No matter, no matter," she said briskly. "Plenty of good schools, and students like you can excel anywhere. If I remember, your second choice was . . . UCLA?"

Beth rubbed her hand against the back of her neck and made a small noise of agreement. She glanced over her shoulder at the door, wishing there was some graceful way she could cut short the conversation and flee.

"And you were accepted, I presume?"

Beth made another noncommittal noise.

"What's that?" Ms. Polansky asked sharply.

"Yes," Beth said, sighing heavily. "I got in."

"Buck up," the teacher told her. "I spent some time in L.A. as a young woman—many, many years ago, as you can imagine—and it's really quite the exotic locale. I'm sure someone like you will have no trouble—"

"I'm not going," Beth admitted. Ripping it off fast, like a Band-Aid. But it still hurt.

"What's that?"

Beth settled into one of the chairs in the front row of the empty classroom, feeling a strange sense of déjà vu, as if any minute Ms. Polansky would start lecturing about

Hamlet's motivations in the third act while Beth struggled not to think about whether Adam would like her dress for the junior prom.

"Some stuff happened this year, and, uh, I turned down my acceptance," Beth said. She didn't say the part about how she'd thought there was no point to planning a future when she couldn't imagine living through the next day. Nor did she mention that she had expected to spend next year lying on a couch with her stoner boyfriend, choking on a cloud of pot that would help her forget everything she was passing up.

"Why would you do a stupid thing like that?" Ms. Polansky snapped.

Beth winced. "I'm just stupid, I guess."

"You're the farthest thing from it." Ms. Polansky settled down at the desk next to her. Her voice softened. "What happened?"

Beth shrugged. "I made a mistake."

"Can you fix it?"

"No." Not that she hadn't tried. Her father had tried. Her guidance counselor had tried. But it was permanent; it was over. "I missed the deadline. They'd still be willing to let me in, but . . . I lost my scholarship. And without it . . ." Beth shrugged again. Without the money, there was no way. She'd always known that. It was the reason she'd worked so hard every day, every year, knowing that her only shot for the future was in being perfect. And she'd actually managed it, right up until the very end. When she'd thrown it all away. "I'm thinking about taking some night classes . . . community college or something. . . ."

Ms. Polansky handed the yearbook back to her and

stood up. "Well, then. That's settled. I'm sure you'll find a way to make it work."

"I'm sorry," Beth said.

"For what?"

"For . . . letting you down."

"Nonsense," the teacher said. "You're only letting yourself down."

That made it even worse.

Harper stuffed a limp, greasy fry in her mouth, washing it down with a swig of flat Diet Coke. "Exactly which part of this are you going to miss?" she asked Miranda, who was gazing at the tacky fluorescent décor like it was the Sistine Chapel.

Miranda squeezed closer to Kane, who was stroking her arm with one hand and stealing fries off her untouched plate with the other. "This," Miranda insisted. *"Us."*

"I see you every day, Rand," Harper pointed out. "And next year, when we get the hell out of here and get our own apartment, I'll see you even more. And as for your boyfriend here"—she jerked her head at Kane—"I could do with seeing him a little less."

"You know you'll miss me next year," Kane said, flashing her a smug grin. "What would you do without me?"

"Celebrate good times," Harper sang tunelessly.

"Your life would be dull and colorless without me," Kane argued.

"Oh, Geary, I know how much you love to be right, so why don't you prove it? You leave and never come back, and I'll e-mail you to let you know how it all turns out."

Kane grabbed a straw from the table, tore off one end

of the wrapper, then brought the straw to his lips and blew the wrapper into Harper's face. "Patience, Grace. All good things come to those who wait."

Harper grinned—then spotted the hint of a quiver in Miranda's lower lip. *Stupid,* she told herself. Miranda had been dreaming about Kane for years, and now that she finally had him, he was headed east to college in less than three months. And Harper just had to dredge it up and turn it into a joke.

"I'll be waiting a long time," she said quickly. "Fall feels like forever away. *Graduation* feels like forever away."

"It's only two weeks," Miranda pointed out, picking at her food. "And I just thought coming back here at least once before it's all over—it would be like the old days."

The Nifty Fifties diner, with its peeling movie posters, and Buddy Holly tunes blasting out of the ancient speakers, was the perfect spot for nostalgia. Especially since they'd been coming here several nights a week since ninth grade. The fab four: Harper, Kane, Miranda—and Adam.

Now Kane and Miranda were nuzzling each other and sharing a shake, while Harper sat on her side of the booth, alone.

"You're such a sap," Harper told her best friend.

"Speaking of which . . ." Miranda pulled out her camera.

"No more!" Harper said, waving her hands in front of her face. Miranda had been documenting everything that had happened for the past couple weeks.

"No way," Kane said, trying to grab the camera out of Miranda's hands. She squirmed away. "No need to immortalize another lame night in the world's lamest diner."

"Come on," Miranda begged. "For me?"

Kane looked at Harper. Harper rolled her eyes. "The things we do for love," she said, spreading her arms in defeat. She waved Kane over to her side of the booth. "Come on, let's get this over with."

Kane squeezed in next to her, and they pressed their heads together. Miranda held up the camera. "Think happy thoughts!"

But as the camera flashed, Harper's mouth dropped open and her eyebrows knit together in alarm, turning her face into a fright mask of shock and horror. Because right before the camera flash had blinded her, she'd glanced toward the door. The perfect couple—blond, bronzed, beautiful—had just walked in. They weren't holding hands, but they were a couple nonetheless. Anyone could see it.

They were heading right for her.

"What's *he* doing here?" Harper spat.

Miranda turned around, then looked back at Harper, eyes wide. "I don't know, I didn't—" She suddenly looked at Kane. "Did you?"

Kane tapped his fingers on the table. "I didn't know he would bring *her*."

"Even so, what were you thinking?" Miranda hissed.

"I was thinking *she* wasn't coming," he whispered, jerking his head toward Harper. "Like you told me."

"Then I told you she *was* coming."

"Well, by then, it was too late, wasn't it?"

"You could have said something," Miranda complained.

"I just did."

"Forget it," Harper snapped. "It doesn't matter. It's

done. I'm out of here." She stood up just as Adam and Beth reached the table. Beth was wearing a pale green, polka-dot sundress with a white sash around the waist that looked like it belonged at a post-golf garden party—but, fashion don't or not, it still showed off her long limbs and deep tan. *Lawn Party Barbie,* Harper thought in disgust. *And she's finally reclaimed her Ken.*

"Harper," Adam said in surprise. "I didn't know you were going to be here."

"I'm not," Harper said. "This is just an optical illusion. It'll be over in a second."

"You don't have to go just because—"

"Yes." She glared at Beth, who at least had the decency to look away. "I do."

Miranda caught up with her just outside the diner, and they stood in the doorway, the flashing neon casting their faces in blue and red. "Don't go," Miranda pleaded.

"I can't sit there and look at the two of them," Harper said. "You know that."

Miranda sighed. "Yeah. I know. I just . . ."

"Rand, we've got plenty of time," Harper told her. "We can make ourselves sick on greasy crap some other night."

"It just feels like everything's . . ." She shook her head. "I only wanted it to be like it was in the old days, for once."

"This isn't the old days," Harper pointed out. "And maybe the old days weren't so great, anyway."

"Maybe." Miranda gave her a sad smile. "Do you want me to leave with you?"

"I'm fine," Harper lied, grabbing her by the shoulders and turning her back toward the entrance. "Stay here with

Kane. Have fun. And if you happen to get the chance to pour boiling coffee in her lap . . ."

Miranda gave her a quick hug. "Call you later. Have a good night."

"Yeah." As if. Miranda went back inside, and Harper began the long walk home. Although it was only a few hours past sunset, the streets were empty, the stores boarded up for the night, and the bars already stuffed with people looking for a quick and cheap escape from the dusty desert night. Walking down the narrow road, the streetlights flickering and the moon hidden behind a cloud, it was easy for Harper to convince herself she was the last person in the world. Or at least the last person who mattered.

Her phone rang when she was only a few blocks from home; she didn't recognize the number. Any other time, she would have screened, but hearing someone else's voice—anyone else's voice—would be better than listening to her own. "Hello?"

"Hey, it's Jake."

She hesitated, trying to connect the name with a face.

"Jake Oberman?" the voice said, and the face became clear. It was a rugged, chiseled face with dark eyes and soft lips, with a shock of dark hair slipping down over the eyes. Jake Oberman, senior, point guard, prom date. Jake Oberman, who had rescued her on the dance floor and then, proving himself the perfect gentlemen, had driven her home, opened the car door for her, walked her to her house, and left with only a quick good night kiss and not a single complaint that she was cutting short their prom date before eleven o'clock.

"Hey," she said warily. "What's up?"

"I'm in town," he said. "In Grace—you know, the Lost and Found?"

"Know it and loathe it."

"Yeah, it's a shithole," Jake agreed. "Which is why I'm getting out. Any chance you want to grab some food?"

"Are you asking me out on a date?" Harper said, a flirtatious tone creeping into her voice. "A little last-minute, don't you think?"

"You aren't one of those Rules girls, are you?" he asked. "Need three days' notice for a date, never call a guy, don't kiss until the third date, all that crap?"

"And what if I am?"

"I'd pretend I didn't think you were a total freak," he said. "After all, I'm a gentleman."

"Right, I can tell," she teased. "But you didn't answer my question. Are you asking me out on a date?"

"What if I am?"

"Then I'd probably wonder what was in it for me."

Jake laughed. She had to admit, he had a good one—hearty, but not forced. And a good, solid baritone, just like his voice. "Free food and the scintillating company of yours truly?"

"Scintillating?" she repeated. "Why, Mr. Oberman, are you trying to impress me with your big SAT words and fancy book learnin'?"

"Whatever works," he said. "So, what do you say?"

She had reached her street. She paused on the curb. Her house was much bigger than Adam's, a holdover from the time when the Grace family had ruled the town. Now it was all her parents could do to make payments on their second mortgage. Adam's house was smaller, but the paint was fresh and the lawn neatly trimmed. He worked hard to make it presentable. In the old days, he had mowed the Grace lawn, too, first for some extra spending money and later for an excuse to hang around shirtless while Harper teased him from the sidelines and brought him fresh lemonade.

"Harper?"

"Sorry? What?"

"You, me, a whirlwind romance?" he prodded her. "Or, you know, a slice of pizza."

A few months ago, Harper would have said yes without a second thought. She'd already dated half the guys in the senior class, and most of them weren't nearly as hot as this Jake guy. Kane had good taste, she'd give him that. It could even be fun—he looked like a jock but talked like a human being, which was always a plus. Besides, back then, none of that would have mattered. Harper felt unwanted, Jake wanted her—it was a simple equation.

"Maybe another night," she said, and now she didn't sound flirtatious, just tired. "Rain check?"

"I'll hold you to that," he said.

She didn't have a witty response, and she didn't care, so she just said good-bye and hung up. And although it was only a few minutes past ten, she went inside and went to bed. Maybe what she'd told Miranda was true. The old days were done.

Beth closed the car door and settled back into the passenger seat with a loud sigh of relief. "Well, that was . . ."

"Awkward." Adam stuck the key in the ignition, trying not to replay the night in his mind. It had been a mistake to bring Beth; it had been a mistake to come in the first place. It had, mostly, been a mistake to think that he could make things normal again, just by wishing it.

"With a capital A," Beth agreed.

"I'm sorry." Adam pulled out of the lot, reminded of all the nights he'd come to the diner to pick up Beth after her shift. Back when she still worked there; back when they were still in love.

"Don't apologize," she said. "They're your friends."

"So are you." He reached over to squeeze her shoulder. "If they can't handle that . . ." No one had said so out loud, of course. Beth and Kane had sniped at each other, Miranda, loyal to the bitter end, had glared silently down at the table, unwilling to engage with the enemy. And Adam had tried to keep up a nonstop stream of meaningless conversation without calling attention to the fact that everyone around him was miserable. It would have been hard enough under normal circumstances, but tonight, still shaken from his encounter with the UC-Riverside coach, Adam wasn't quite at his best. He hadn't told anyone about the offer; he still wasn't sure he believed it.

"I know," she said quietly. "Thank you." He laid his hand over hers, and she squeezed it. "It means a lot, that you're always there for me."

Not always, he thought, self-hatred rising like bile. *Not when you needed me.* He saw her there again, standing on the ledge, staring down into the darkness, ready to jump.

An old Simon and Garfunkel song came on the radio, and Adam turned it up.

"I love this song," Beth said, smiling faintly.

"I remember."

"Reed always used to make fun of me for liking this kind of stuff, but . . . sorry."

He glanced over at her, then back at the road. "What?"

"I shouldn't talk about him, with you. I mean, it's kind of weird, right?"

Adam shrugged. "Maybe. But not bad-weird. You should talk about him. If you want."

"I don't."

They listened to the music. Beth sang along under her breath. Her voice was a little thin, but sweet and on key, just as he remembered.

"Okay," he said eventually, pulling the car up to the curb in front of her house. "Door-to-door service."

"Thanks for—you know, thanks," she muttered, fumbling with her seat belt and scooping her bag off the floor.

Adam turned the car off. "Beth, wait." Before, when they were together, she had always pushed him to think about the future. She had wanted better for him than the life he'd planned for himself. And she had always given him the best advice. "Something happened this morning, and uh . . . can I ask you something?"

"Anything." She tucked a strand of hair behind her ear.

"I got called down to the guidance office," he began hesitantly, "and there was this guy there, with the coach. . . ."

She nodded, waiting for him to continue.

But he couldn't. She was depending on him. He could see it in her face. If he was going to leave, he would have to tell her in the right way, at the right time, and this wasn't it. He couldn't say anything, not until he'd made his decision.

"Never mind," he said.

"What? You can tell me."

"No, it's just some stupid basketball thing. It's no big deal. So, I guess, have a good night, okay?"

"Ad, I know you don't want me to thank you anymore, but—" Beth leaned across the seat and gave him a tight hug. He rested his chin on her shoulder and listened to her breathing. "I owe you," she whispered. "For everything."

She let go, but he held on, pulling away only enough to see her face. It was mostly hidden in shadow. There was a tear clinging to the corner of her left eye. She gave him a half smile. "Déjà vu, right?"

He knew that she was thinking of all the nights he'd dropped her off at home, lingering in the car for one last kiss.

"A lot's changed," he said softly. "But . . ."

"It still feels kind of . . ."

"Yeah."

Beth's eyes were watering. These days, they always were. He could almost see the old woman she would become someday, the worry lines and creases, the sagging of time weighing her down. She wasn't the same girl he'd been in love with. If he'd even been in love. She was watching him, like she was waiting for something.

So he kissed her.

It was light, it was hesitant, and then, almost as quickly, it was over.

She pulled away from him, but not in anger. Just surprise. "What was—?"

"I don't know," Adam said quickly. "I just thought . . ."

"You mean you want to . . . ?"

"I don't know." Adam looked down at his hands. One of them was resting next to hers, and he inched it over until their pinkies were interlocked, just like he always used to. "Do you?"

"I don't know." She pulled her hand away and started rubbing her thumb across her palm, the way she did when she was nervous. "I mean . . . we could. I guess. If you wanted to."

He had stopped asking himself what he wanted. Because if he couldn't have what he *really* wanted, then what did it matter anymore?

"Maybe we should just, uh, figure it out later," Adam said.

"Okay. I'm, um, I'm just going to go, then." Beth opened the door, then turned back to him. He leaned toward her to give her another hug, but she went in for a kiss, and their foreheads knocked against each other. Beth looked horrified—then started to giggle. Soon they were both laughing. "Okay, I'm really going now," Beth said, gasping for breath. It was good to see her smile again.

"Good night." He gave her a kiss on the cheek, and she left. He waited until she was safely in the house. Then he flopped forward, letting his head thud against the steering wheel. "What are you doing, Morgan?" he groaned. "What the hell are you doing now?"

chapter

4

In the old days, Beth woke at 6 a.m. every day, weekends included. There was always too much work to sleep, too many obligations clogging her day to enjoy lounging around in bed until noon the way all of her friends did. But now she didn't care about her work and she'd ditched most of her obligations. There didn't seem to be much point anymore to the whole bright-eyed-and-bushy-tailed act, especially when she dreaded nothing more than the prospect of facing another day. Now Beth stayed in bed as long as possible, persuading herself to get up only by promising that, before long, night would fall and she'd be able to climb back in again. So when the phone rang at 9 a.m. on Saturday, she was still sound asleep.

Her friends would have been shocked—if she'd had any left.

"This is Ashley Statten, from the *Grace Weekly Journal*," the woman said, her voice snappy and staccato, each consonant bitten off sharply to make way for the next. "Is this Beth Manning?"

Her first thought was that someone had talked.

So many people knew her secret, and too many of them hated her. Harper had promised she wouldn't say anything to anyone, but . . . Harper had made a lot of promises. And to date, the only one she'd come through on was her promise to ruin Beth's life. So maybe it had only been a matter of time. And if the newspaper had the story, that meant that the police were probably on their way.

She expected terror to shoot through her, but all she felt was a nearly giddy relief. Maybe it was actually over. She'd thought she would have to carry this burden for the rest of her life—just make it through one day, Harper had said, up on the roof, then make it through the next, but that was easier said than done. She hadn't had the nerve to end things herself, but maybe if the police did it for her—

No. Beth had promised herself she would stop thinking like that. She'd promised Adam.

"Some English teacher from your school called, said you're looking for an internship next year," Ashley Statten continued. "We usually don't do that kind of thing, but I guess your teacher used to be my editor's teacher and he's still scared of her, because he didn't say no." She said all this without pausing for breath, and it took a moment for Beth to catch up. "So here's the deal. This is your lucky morning: You get a trial run, because I'm working on the perfect article for you and I could use some backup. You interested?"

"I, uh . . ." Beth rubbed the sleep out of her eyes and tried to process. "Interested in what?"

"A little slow on the uptake, aren't you?" the woman snapped. "I'm working on an article, the anthropology of high school girls, alpha queens and their beta ladies-in-waiting, soft bullying, climbing the social hierarchy, sort of a *Mean Girls* meets *Coming of Age in Samoa*, with a little of that *Ophelia Speaks* crap thrown in for good measure, the seamy underbelly of America's youth, hometown high jinks, et cetera, et cetera, you get the idea, right?"

"Um, right . . ."

"You don't sound too sure."

"Right," Beth said firmly, scrabbling for a pen to write down *Coming of Age in Samoa* so that once she hung up, she could figure out what the woman was talking about.

"So you help me out on this story, be my inside man, so to speak, and then we'll see what we can do about next year."

"Next year?"

"Full-time, paid internship at the glorious *Grace Weekly Journal*," Ashley Statten said sarcastically. "Your entrée into the fabulous world of dead-end, small-town journalism—obituaries, housewife gossip, town meetings about whether to tear down the old Crenshaw place, and epic arguments about gas station zoning permits and land use. Work hard and don't screw up, and all this and more could be yours. You in?"

"Yes!" And for the first time in a long time—since before Kaia, since before Adam had broken her heart and Kane had stomped it to bits, maybe since before Mr. Powell had jumped her in the school newspaper office—Beth let herself imagine a future of ink-stained fingers and tight deadlines, rolling presses, last-minute scoops, secret sources, banner headlines, and a byline, a *real, professional* byline, of her very own.

Beth Manning.

Staff Writer.

Grace Weekly Journal.

It wasn't Berkeley. But it was something; it was a start.

"I'm definitely in," she said eagerly. "Whatever you want, I can handle it. Just tell me what I need to do."

The shapeless black robe made her look like a chocolate doughnut. Miranda shifted toward the right, then to the left, then turned her back to the mirror, craning her head around to try to get a look at her ass. It was undetectable beneath the billowing polyester. That was one good thing, at least—the robe might cover up all the places she went in, but it would also hide the many places she bulged out.

Miranda told herself to stop.

She wasn't supposed to look like a supermodel; she was supposed to look like a graduate.

She arranged the flat-topped cap on her head, flipped the tassel to the left side, and looked again, feeling like she was wearing a costume.

"Oh, you're all grown up!" her mother cried, stepping into the room without knocking. "I don't believe it."

"Believe it, Mom." Miranda rolled her eyes, but she couldn't stop herself from smiling. Was her mother actually experiencing a maternal moment? Unlikely. And yet, that was without question a tissue in her hands, and she was dabbing away at her eyes. Just like a real mother who cared. "Two weeks and I'm out."·

"You know, your father and I are just so proud of you,"

her mother said, coming over to rub Miranda's shoulders. Miranda pulled away. "Our little girl, so smart, so independent, and in the Cal State honors program next year! I have to admit, dear, I had no idea you were so bright."

"I got that," Miranda muttered, taking off her cap and placing it carefully on top of her dresser. She left the robe on. Something about it made her feel powerful, like she could withstand her mother. Or maybe it just gave her a place to hide.

"College is such an enormous step," her mother said kindly. She sat down on Miranda's bed and patted the spot next to her, gesturing for her daughter to sit down too. Miranda stood. "You must be pretty nervous."

Miranda shrugged. "Not really."

"Living on your own for the first time . . ." Her mother shook her head. "It's hard. And not just financially. Maybe if you were more independent, I wouldn't worry so much, but . . ."

"Mom, I've got homework to do, so unless there's something you need—"

"I just need my oldest daughter to be happy," her mother said. "And I've been wondering: Have you given any thought to living at home for another year?"

"*What?*"

"Think about it, Miranda. You don't know how to live on your own. You can commute to classes for a year, and live here, for free, and that way you'll still get to see us, and you can still take care of your little sister in the evenings and help out around the house—"

"You want me to ditch college so that I can be your *nanny*?" Miranda asked incredulously. "I'm supposed to junk my life so that you and Dad can keep having 'date night' twice a week?"

"That's an awful thing to say," her mother said. "I'm thinking about *you*."

"You're never thinking about me," Miranda snapped. "You just don't want to lose your servant next year—who else is going to cook dinner and vacuum and do the laundry? Not Stacy, I know that. And not *you*. This is so selfish."

"Don't talk like that," her mother said. "You may think you're all grown up, but I'm still your mother, and this is still your family, and—" She broke off, dabbing at her eyes again to wipe away some fake tears. "And we need you *here*, at least for a little longer. I don't see what's wrong with that. With my new promotion I'm going to be working longer hours, and your sister isn't old enough yet to stay home on her own. We're your family, and we need you— so you tell me: Who's the selfish one?"

Miranda couldn't speak. She was too angry—except for the tiny part of her that wondered if her mother was right.

"Honey, I didn't come in here to fight," her mother said in a more conciliatory tone. "I just want you to think about it. I really think it would be best for you. You've got some more growing up to do, and the thought of you out there on your own—"

"I won't be on my own," Miranda countered. "I'll be with Harper. We're supposed to be going apartment hunting tomorrow, and you want me to just abandon her?"

"She'd do it to you," her mother said harshly.

"What's that supposed to mean?"

"I see more than you think I see." Her mother scowled.

"I know what kind of a friend that girl's been to you. What happens next time she pulls another one of her stunts, and you're out there all alone?"

"Just stop. Harper's not going to be pulling any *stunts*." Miranda took a deep, calming breath, but it wasn't quite calming enough. "Can you just leave now? I have work to do."

"I'm not leaving until you admit that I only want the best for you, and agree to think about what I said."

"Fine."

"I don't think you understand how much I've had to sacrifice for you, Miranda, how much I've given up to be a good mother to you, and I don't think it's untoward of me to ask you to make a small sacrifice for me, for your family. I don't think that's out of line."

"I said *fine*. Fine!"

"You'll think about it?"

Miranda sighed. "I'll think about it."

Her mother stood up and walked over to the door, pausing on her way out. "You really do look lovely in your robe, darling."

"Thanks," Miranda said warily.

"I know how you girls are at this age: You hate things that seem loose and shapeless, but there are times when that can be more a blessing than a curse—am I right?"

"What are you getting at, Mom?"

"Nothing!" she protested. "How about this weekend we go shopping for something special to wear underneath it. A new dress."

"That's okay," Miranda said. "I'm going with Harper."

Her mother raised her eyebrows. "I assume she's the one who let you buy that prom dress?"

"What was wrong with my dress?"

"Nothing . . ."

"But," Miranda prompted her.

"But I just think that you would have looked better in something that wasn't quite so clingy. If you would just let me help you, I could teach you how to cover up your problem areas rather than draw attention to them like—"

"Forget it!" Miranda snapped. "Just let it go. Please."

"You've never been grateful for anything I've tried to do for you," her mother said in exasperation. "I'll just never understand how I raised such an impolite child. You accuse me of only thinking about myself, dear—I suggest you take a look in the mirror."

And when her mother was finally, blissfully gone, Miranda did exactly that.

Not a doughnut, she thought in disgust. *I look like a bonbon. A short, round, bulgy, chocolate bonbon.*

Miranda ripped off the gown and threw herself down on the bed, reaching for the bag of mini Snickers she'd stashed beneath it for emergencies like this one. Talking to her mother opened up a gaping hole inside her, one that could only be filled by massive amounts of gooey chocolate. So much chocolate, in the end, that she would balloon out into the disgusting round mess that her mother saw whenever she looked at her; so much chocolate that she would feel sick, and bloated, and need more than anything to get it out of her, to stick her finger down her throat and lean over the toilet with the faucet running so no one would hear, and choke out all the calories and sugar and words that were weighing her down.

She had promised herself she wasn't going to do it anymore; she had promised Harper.

And if that wasn't enough, there was the thought of Kane. If he ever knew what she did when she was alone and miserable—if he ever saw her hunched over, face pale and sweaty, stomach clenched, choking on the stench, stuffing the empty candy wrappers into her backpack and then throwing them out in the garbage can down the street so that no one, especially her prying, judging, hating mother, would ever know—Kane would be disgusted. Because it was disgusting. *She* was disgusting.

Just one, she thought to herself. *I'll just eat one, or maybe two.* And then she would call Kane, or Harper, and get out of the house. She pulled a candy bar from the bag, tore off the wrapper, and bit into the gooey sweetness. The caramel filling stuck to her teeth, and the rich taste cut through her confusion. She wouldn't think about her mother anymore, or about next year, or the apartment, or how helping her family meant abandoning Harper but keeping her promise to Harper meant abandoning her family. In fact, she wouldn't think at all. She would just taste, and chew, and swallow.

Only one. Maybe two, she told herself, tearing into the second bar even as she chomped down on the first. *Then I'm done.*

Adam faked left, went right, raced for the foul line, and got off a perfect shot. He followed the graceful arc toward the basket—and even Kane had to nod in appreciation at the soft swish.

"Nice. Been practicing, Morgan?" Kane asked, grabbing

the rebound. "Waste of time—you know you'll never beat me."

And, in all their years of playing one-on-one, he never had. Adam lunged for Kane, knocking the ball out of his hands and stealing possession. He imagined a horde of screaming fans on the sideline rising to their feet and holding their breath in anticipation as he dribbled downcourt, heart pounding, feet slapping the concrete, the ball stinging his fingers as he slapped it down again, and then stopped, rising to his toes, cradling the ball in his fingertips, tensing his muscles, bending his knees, aiming and, all in a single graceful move, a split second that left no time for thought, only action, thrusting the ball into the air for three perfect, final, game-winning points.

Kane leaped up, slapped the ball away from the basket, cradled it to his chest and, two dribbles later, sunk an easy layup. "That's twenty-one." He passed the ball to Adam, hard. "Game."

"Maybe I let you win," Adam said, grabbing his shirt and water bottle. He twisted off the cap and gulped down a few mouthfuls, almost choking. The sun had turned it into a hot soup. He gave up on drinking and poured the rest of it over his head, closing his eyes as the water splashed across his face and ran down his chest, washing away the sweat. He felt good. Exhausted, overheated, thirsty, defeated—but good. "Maybe I've been letting you win the whole time."

"Then maybe you're a bigger moron than I thought."

"Good game," Adam said, tossing over Kane's water bottle without bothering to warn him of the putrid temperature.

"Good for me," Kane shot back. He tipped the bottle back over his mouth and, watching Adam out of the corner of his eye, downed the whole thing in nearly one gulp.

They headed for the parking lot, empty except for Kane's lavishly restored silver Camaro and Adam's beat-up Chevrolet, both parked in the only shade. Adam leaned against the door of his car, the one that was painted a different color than the rest. He was in no hurry to get home.

"I'm gonna miss this," he said.

Kane hopped up on the hood of the Camaro and stretched out like a cat in the sun. "Losing? Don't worry, Morgan, there'll be plenty of opportunity for that."

Adam threw his sweaty T-shirt at Kane's face. *"This,"* he said. "Playing ball here." He gestured over to the other end of the lot, where the empty high school waited for Monday to arrive and its inmates to return. "I might even miss that."

"Drink some more water, man," Kane teased. "You must have sunstroke."

Adam laughed. "Okay. But at least this."

"Dude, don't cry. We've got all summer. Time enough for me to beat you hundreds of times."

"Maybe not," Adam said.

"How many times do you need to lose before you stop denying the inevitable?"

"Not that," Adam said, rolling his eyes. "I mean, I might not be around all summer. I might have to take off early ... for training."

Kane sat up. "You joining the marines?"

It had just slipped out. But now that it had, Adam didn't want to stop himself. He had to tell someone. "Some coach from UC-Riverside wants to recruit me," he admitted. "Admission, scholarship, a spot on the team—I've got until graduation to decide. Less than two weeks. And if I say yes, I go in July to work out with the team and start some work-study job."

"Are you kidding me?" Kane jumped off the car and slapped his fist against Adam's. "Awesome."

Adam shrugged.

"Wait—what do you mean *if* you say yes?" Kane asked, narrowing his eyes.

"I mean, *if*." Adam leaned back, searching the sky for clouds. He couldn't find any. "I don't know if I want to go."

"You don't know if you want to go to a *real* college, for free, and play on a division-one team?"

"Borrega's a real college," Adam said hotly. "Real enough for me, at least. I know it's not *Penn State*"—he scowled—"but we can't all be brainiacs like you."

"For one thing, you're not as dumb as you pretend to be," Kane said. "Otherwise I wouldn't be wasting my Saturday with you."

"I must be even *dumber* than I pretend to be," Adam countered. "Otherwise I wouldn't be wasting my Saturday with you."

"Very funny." Kane didn't crack a smile. "So what's the deal? Why do you need two weeks to figure this one out? You shouldn't need two minutes."

"It's complicated," Adam said. "It's far away, and my mom doesn't have anyone else, and it'd be a lot of work and, you know. There's Harper. And Beth."

Kane shook his head in disgust. "Wrong answer."

"What do you want me to say? It's the truth."

"Morgan, what are you doing? You want to be with Harper? Be with Harper. You want to be with Beth—well, that's your mental problem—suck it up and be with Beth. But either way, they're just *girls*—pick one, pick the other one, fine, but don't waste your whole life sticking around for them."

"It's not that simple," Adam said. "You don't know—"

"Hey, I got a girlfriend now. You don't see me ditching Penn State for Stevens, do you?"

"It's different," Adam insisted. "You and Miranda . . ."

"What?"

"Nothing." Kane would never understand what it meant to care about someone; what it meant to have someone depend on you.

"Fine. Forget it. Back to you and your screwed-up life," Kane said, when it became obvious Adam wasn't going to elaborate. "You're telling me you'd give this up for Harper? It's not like you're willing to give up anything *else* for her."

"Don't—" Adam broke off, feeling the anger bubbling in him again. But it wasn't directed at Kane. "You don't know what's going on with the two of us, so don't—don't talk about it."

"I know she's miserable," Kane said. "And you're prancing around with Beth like you don't give a shit."

"Well, I do, okay?" Adam said angrily.

"So freaking do something about it."

"Don't you think I want to?" Adam kicked at his junky car door. It shook with the impact. "I can't."

Kane blew out a short, dismissive breath. "Because of Beth."

"Yeah." Adam slumped back against the car. "Because of Beth."

She hadn't intended to eavesdrop.

She'd just wanted to share her good news—and she wanted to do it without Kane's sneer getting in the way.

Beth had spent the morning in the *Grace Weekly Journal* offices, gaping at the people running back and forth—even on a Saturday—to put together a *real* newspaper. So, okay, there were only three staffers, and the big breaking story was a water main leak on Azure Avenue, but it was a newspaper. And she was a part of it. Ashley Statten, a miniscule woman with a bleached-blond pixie cut and big brown eyes, had given her the rundown of her story—talking even faster than she had on the phone—and then gave Beth her assignment. She was to interview her fellow students and find out, in Ashley's words, "what they want, what they need, who they really are, deep down, where no one can see." If she did it well, she might actually be able to fix the mess she'd made of her future. Next year didn't have to be one long, hideous shift at Guido's pizza parlor, shirking from Reed's hostile gaze and wondering whether the grease would ever wash out of her hair.

And all she'd wanted to do was celebrate it with someone. The newspaper office was only a few blocks from the high school, from the basketball court where Adam played pickup ball every Saturday, so she'd walked over, planning to surprise him. And instead, here she was, hiding behind a tree like some kind of feeble cartoon character, waiting for Kane to leave . . . and listening.

"You don't owe her anything," Kane said. "And if she's trying to tell you different—"

"She's not telling me anything. She just needs me."

Kane peered intently at him, then burst into laughter.

"What?" Adam asked.

"You *are* a moron," Kane said, shaking his head. "Unbelievable."

"What?"

"You're hooking up with her, aren't you?" Kane started laughing again.

"Am not," Adam said.

"Come on, Morgan, there's a reason I always clean you out when we play poker."

"It was just one time," Adam admitted. "We didn't even . . ."

Kane bowed with a flourish. "Never bluff the master," he crowed. "So what now? You're getting back together?"

Adam didn't say anything for a moment. He rubbed his forehead with the heel of his hand. "I don't know. Maybe?"

"You know what your problem is?" Kane asked, opening his trunk and tossing in the basketball.

"You?"

"You've got a hero complex. You see a damsel in distress, you think it's your job to rescue her. You don't know how to be with a girl if you're not rescuing her from something."

"I never had to rescue Harper," Adam said defensively.

Kane gave him a pointed look. "Exactly."

Adam opened his car door, glaring. "You have no idea what you're talking about." He got into the driver's seat, but Kane grabbed the door before Adam could shut it.

"I know you feel sorry for her," he said. "Hell, even *I* feel sorry for her. It's pathetic. But that doesn't mean you owe her anything."

"She's my friend," Adam said stubbornly. "She needs me."

"If that's true, she won't want you screwing up your life for her. Maybe she's not as needy as you think." Kane slammed the door shut, then got into his own car, and they both pulled out of the lot.

Beth leaned back against the tree, then let herself slide down to the ground, the bark scraping her back.

She had known that Adam felt sorry for her. But she'd let herself believe that he was telling the truth when he said he'd stood by her because he wanted to, because he cared. The other night in his car, she had even let herself believe that there was still something between them, or could be.

It was pathetic. Kane was right: *She* was pathetic. And she was dragging Adam down because she was too weak to convince him to walk away.

Tomorrow, she thought with determination. *I'll tell him tomorrow.* She would persuade him that she was strong, that she didn't need his support. She would convince him that he would be better off far away from her. And whatever came next, she would face it.

Alone.

chapter

5

"This dump is even worse than the last place," Miranda hissed, pulling Harper out of the apartment so she could breathe again without choking on the stench.

"It's not so bad," Harper argued. "It could use some cleaning up, sure, but it was a good space, and the building's kind of . . . well, it's got character."

Miranda looked from the peeling paint to the mold-encrusted ceilings to the stained carpet that smelled faintly of urine, and finally back to Harper. "I think you mean it's got character*s*," she said. "As in, scary guys in chains hanging out on the front stoop who look like characters from *The Sopranos*."

Harper rolled her eyes and headed down the hallway, toward the narrow, musky fire-stairs. There was an elevator, but according to the dirt-encrusted sign on the front—the one that looked like it had been hanging there for years—it was out of order. "I don't think we need to worry too much about the Jersey mob if we live here."

"Oh, there's no *if*," Miranda said firmly. "This half of *we* will under no circumstances be living *here*."

"What about the last place we saw?" Harper asked, once they were safely back out on the street.

Miranda shook her head. "That stain . . ."

"I told you, it wasn't blood," Harper insisted.

"Says you."

"So what about the third place?"

Miranda wrinkled her nose. "Was that the one with the shower in the kitchen or the one that smelled like the town dump and was next to the local Hells Angels head-quarters?"

"Shower in kitchen," Harper murmured.

"No."

"Then what—"

"And no to the Hells Angel's place too," Miranda said quickly. They turned left onto the main avenue, and the campus opened up before them, all sprawling green lawns and Spanish-style stucco buildings, with real college students hurrying back and forth, backpacks slung over their shoulders, cell phones—or, in some cases, Frisbees—in hand.

"College," Miranda said in amazement. "Can you believe it? This is really going to be us next year."

"Not if you don't stop vetoing all our apartment options," Harper said.

"Find me a place that doesn't suck," Miranda said, "and I won't veto it." Nor would she sign a lease, not until she decided whether she was moving at all, or giving in to her mother's wishes. But what Harper didn't know couldn't hurt Miranda.

Harper waved a copy of the local newspaper in her face. "We've seen every place we can afford, and they're all beneath your standards. You think *I* want to live in one of these piles of crap?"

"It's almost enough to make you want to stay in Grace," Miranda said, laughing nervously. "You know, live at home for a year, save up some money for a real place. One that doesn't have a pee-stained rug and a meth lab on the fourth floor."

"Please, god, tell me you're joking." Harper plopped down on a nearby bench and flung her arms out dramatically. "Tell me you haven't forgotten our sacred vow to get the hell out of Grace as fast as humanly possible."

Miranda gave her a weak smile. And then her phone rang.

"Hello?" she said, glad for the interruption.

"Hey, gorgeous, any luck finding a palace fit for a queen?"

Miranda smiled, blushing, happy Kane couldn't see her through the phone. It was bad enough having Harper there, batting her eyelashes and fluttering a hand over her heart. "Tell your *lover* I say hello," she whispered, a wicked grin on her face. Miranda turned to face the other direction.

"Maybe if I were the queen of the underworld," she said into the phone, sighing. "It turns out hunting for affordable student housing is the ninth circle of hell."

"That's what you get for picking a school without dorms," he teased. "You'll be squeezed into some apartment too tiny for a decent-size keg, while I'll be . . . well, let's just say they don't call it Happy Valley for nothing."

"So I should be back in a few hours," Miranda said abruptly. She didn't like to think about what would happen next year, when Kane would move three thousand miles away. "What time are you picking me up?"

"Uh, yeah, that's actually why I'm calling," Kane said. "I'm going to have to cancel—something came up."

"Oh." Miranda resisted the urge to ask him what. If he wanted her to know, he would tell her. But he didn't.

"Sorry about this," he said. "I know I promised you we'd finally hit that Mexican place you love, but—"

"Another time," she said, trying to sound like she didn't care. And like this wasn't the fourth time in three weeks he'd cancelled like this, abruptly, mysteriously . . . suspiciously.

"Maybe tomorrow?"

"Maybe." She grinned. "Unless I get a better offer."

"They don't come much better than me," he boasted.

"I'm trying a new thing this week," she said. "Optimism. So I'd like to believe there's still hope."

"There's always hope, Stevens. I'll keep my fingers crossed for you. Sorry again about tonight."

"No problem. Later."

She hung up the phone and gave Harper a rueful smile. "So it looks like I don't have to go back early after all."

"He cancelled?"

Miranda nodded.

"Again?"

Another nod.

"With no explanation, I assume?"

Miranda slumped down on the bench next to Harper. "Tell me he's not seeing someone else."

"He's not seeing someone else," Harper repeated dutifully.

"You believe that?"

Harper paused. "I believe it if you do." Then she swatted Miranda with the rolled-up newspaper. "Look on the bright side, Rand. This means we get to look at more apartments."

Miranda grimaced. "And the day just keeps getting better and better."

"Goddamnit!" Reed smashed another bottle against the brick. Impact. The bottle exploded. Glass skidded and swooped through the air, clattering onto the hard-packed dirt. He didn't feel any better.

He never felt any better.

He let himself slouch to the ground. Then he fell back, head thudding into the overgrown grass, arms stretched out. A snow angel. If there were ever any snow. He closed his eyes. It was like snow in his mind. A foggy white dust speckled over his thoughts, burying them in the deep. They jutted up, smooth white shapes, evidence of what had been.

Lost the job.

Lost Kaia.

Lost Beth.

Lost everything.

The pain was still there, still sharp, like someone was taking a baseball bat to his stomach. But he couldn't attach it to anything that had happened or anything that he'd done. It was just there, along with the rage, along with the misery. There without cause, without purpose, and without end.

If he could see the problems—if he could dig his life out of the snow, see it clear again, maybe there would be something to fix. But the way things were, it seemed point-less. Everything seemed pointless. Better to let the snow bury him.

"Dude, what the hell?"

Reed opened his eyes.

A pale apparition loomed over him, blond hair shim-mering down.

"Beth?"

An explosion of laughter.

"He thinks you're his girlfriend!" Another body appeared, shoved the first one out of the way. They landed on the ground. Reed closed his eyes again, shut them out. "Dude, you're wasted."

"Am not," Reed mumbled.

Wasted.

That was the word. Everything had been wasted, had wasted away. He'd thrown it away. Or she had thrown it away. He couldn't remember which anymore. Didn't care.

Hands grabbed his shoulders, dragged him up. He stepped, stumbled, lurched, fell again. Arms caught him. Held tight.

"To the couch," someone said. "Help me get him inside."

His feet scuffed across the grass, smearing through the dirt. Reed laughed, though he didn't know why.

"Funny for you, man. You're not the one doing the heavy lifting."

"'s not funny," he slurred. "Sucks. It sucks." The world was too bright, and he was too dizzy. It was better with his eyes closed, when he could wish the lurching, sickening motion away. "Leggo!" he cried suddenly, lashing out. His arm thudded into something with a soft thwap, and someone grunted. Let go. And he sank to the side, almost dropping to the ground, where it was solid and it was still. But then they gripped again, tighter this time, and he was moving.

"Yeah, it sucks," someone said. "At least you got that part right."

They dropped him, and it was soft, and it was cool, and finally, he slept.

"Remember the first time we came out here?" Miranda asked, sipping her Diet Coke.

Harper started laughing so suddenly, she nearly choked on her grilled cheese. "Visiting Kane's brother," she said, after she'd swallowed. "Big man on campus. We thought we were *so* cool, going to our first real college party."

"Party. Right." Miranda giggled.

"There were people and music," Harper said defensively. "That's technically a party."

"People lying on the floor stoned out of their minds," Miranda reminded her. "And lots of Bob Marley."

"You tried pot for the first time."

"And you drank so many wine coolers, you threw up in a bush."

Harper shivered in horror. "I almost puked on Adam—he got out of the way just in time. Not such a successful outing."

"You did hook up with that college guy," Miranda said. "What was his name? Peter? Paul?"

Soda spurted out of Harper's nose. "Patrick!" she exclaimed. "Poor, poor Patrick, with his pierced tongue and his organic deodorant. I couldn't get his stink off me for days."

Miranda sighed. "Things were good back then, weren't they?"

Harper took another bite of her grilled cheese, the house specialty. "What's with all the nostalgia trips, Rand?"

"I don't know. It's just a lot, all at once, you know?"

Harper gave her an exasperated look. "Obviously I don't know, or I wouldn't be asking."

"Hello, graduation? Ring a bell? End of high school, beginning of college, everyone's going away, everything's changing."

"Not everything," Harper counted. "I mean, I know Kane—"

"I don't want to talk about it," Miranda said.

"Okay. Fine. My point is, the rest of us are all sticking around here. Everyone that counts. You. Me."

"Adam?"

"Now I don't want to talk about it," Harper said.

"Fine."

They sat in silence as the waitress took their plates away and brought over the thick slices of chocolate cake Harper had insisted they order. Another specialty of the house. Harper dug right in and, after a moment of hesitation, Miranda followed suit.

"So if every topic is off-limits now, does that mean we're not going to talk at all?" Miranda finally asked.

"Not every topic," Harper said. "Apartments." She pulled out the flyer from the last place they'd seen, a cozy two bedroom a few blocks from campus. "This is it. Big windows, okay kitchen, the shower's in the bathroom where it belongs—and bonus, it doesn't smell like dead bodies. I think we should go back and sign the lease before someone else gets it."

"Harper, I told you, I'm not ready yet."

"But what are you waiting for?" Harper asked, irritated. It was, by far, the best place they'd seen all day—and despite her massive flirting offensive, the owner had offered no assurance that he'd hold it for them. "You need extra time to find something wrong with it? Look, I'll even let you have the bigger bedroom." Then Harper imagined stuffing all of her clothes into the tiny closet. "Well, I'll flip you for it. That's only fair."

Miranda just took another bite of her cake.

"What? *What?* Am I missing something? Tell me what's wrong with it."

"Nothing's wrong with it," Miranda said. "It's great. I can totally see living there with you. But the thing is . . ."

Harper's throat clenched as she waited for Miranda to finish, knowing this couldn't possibly be good.

"My mom wants me to stay home for the year, find a way to commute," Miranda finally said, staring down at her plate. "She just got some big promotion, and she needs help taking care of Stacy, and you know I'm like their free babysitting service, and she laid this big guilt trip on me about how I was abandoning the family and—"

"And you told her she's a selfish bitch and you've wasted enough of your life doing what she wants," Harper finished for her, without much hope.

"And I told her I'd think about it," Miranda admitted.

Harper slumped down on the table, resting her forehead against the cool plastic—at least until she remembered where she was and decided that even dramatic effect wasn't worth physical contact with the million germs skittering across the grimy surface. "Why would you do that?" she moaned, sitting up.

"Because she said it was important," Miranda said. "That she really needs me."

"Where was she when you needed her?"

"Needed her for what?"

"Oh, I don't know. How about needed her to be an actual mother and *not* make you feel like shit every time she opened her mouth?"

"She's not that bad," Miranda said.

"She's worse."

"Look, I haven't made any decisions one way or another."

Harper exploded. "You shouldn't even have a decision to make! You promised me that you were coming next year—we had it all planned out. We're going to Cal State, we're getting an apartment. We have a *plan*. You can't just flake out at the last minute!"

"Stop yelling at me!" Miranda cried. "I'm not doing this to screw you over—" She stopped herself and took a couple deep breaths. "Look, I'm not doing anything at all, okay? Not yet." She stood up. "I'm going to the bathroom, okay? Try to chill out."

Harper looked up at Miranda, then pointedly down at the chocolate crumbs on her empty plate. "Rand, you promised you weren't going to do that anymore."

"What?"

"I'm sorry I yelled at you." Harper tried to look apologetic, even though inside she was still seething. "I didn't mean to get you so upset that you . . . look, you promised to stop, okay?"

Miranda tried to turn away, but Harper grabbed her wrist.

"Promised to stop what?"

Harper tried to stifle her irritation. This was so typical of Miranda, running off to bend over a toilet rather than actually dealing. "You know what I mean," she said, not wanting to spell out all the gross details.

"I'm going. To. The. Bathroom." Miranda spoke slowly and clearly. "It's not a euphemism."

Harper gave her a skeptical look.

"What, you want to come with me and stand outside the stall?" Miranda waited a moment, then shrugged. "Didn't think so. I'll be back in a minute. Don't skip out and stick me with the bill."

Harper smiled sweetly. "Would I ever do that to you?"

Miranda raised her eyebrow—a nasty habit she'd picked up from Kane, who could, of course, say everything he ever needed to with the arch of a single brow. It drove Harper crazy.

Harper sighed. "Rand, you know I'm not going anywhere. We're in this together."

"And by 'this,' you mean . . . ?"

"Whatever happens next," Harper said.

"So that means I'm stuck with you?"

"For life."

Miranda burst into laughter. "*Now* I feel like throwing up."

Harper kept the smile on her face until Miranda was safely behind the bathroom door. Then it fell away. *She* was the one who felt like throwing up, and not through some perverse need to purge herself of chocolate cake. Miranda was right: Everything *was* changing.

Which, now that she thought of it, seemed like an incredibly obvious and overdue observation. But she hadn't given it much thought. As long as Miranda was around, Harper could pretend things were the same as they always were—that *she* was the same as always. But on her own . . .

She was Harper Grace, scion of the Grace family, heir to a proud heritage of haughtiness, social power, lost treasure, and former glory. She was Harper Grace, prom queen, alpha female, arbiter of all things cool, most desired, most likely to get whatever she wanted, no matter who got hurt along the way. She was Harper Grace, the girl to be envied, the girl who saw what she needed and took it, the girl with the power.

Or at least she was—within the confines of Grace, California, where sophomores worshipped her, bartenders sucked up to her, boys chased her. Where everyone knew who she was and what she stood for.

Who was she here, a hundred miles away, in a town full of strangers? As long as Miranda was by her side, she was still everything she'd ever been. But alone? She could be anyone; she could be no one.

The call came an hour late, but at least it came.

Kane grabbed his coat and keys and drove out to the rendezvous point, a secluded alley on the edges of town, behind a bar that had closed its doors a year before. The space had never been sold to anyone else, so it sat dark and empty, just waiting for shady characters to show up and conduct their shady business. It was safe and secluded, but mostly, Kane liked it because it established the appropriate atmosphere. It was his second favorite thing about this whole business: the ominous darkness, the way it made him feel edgy and dangerous and completely in control.

His most favorite thing, of course, was the money.

And it was rolling in.

His San Francisco connection had come through, and the shipments of pot candy—Buddafingers, Puff-a-Mint Patties, Rasta Reese's, an infinite variety of chocolate delights—came through every week, right on schedule, arriving in unmarked boxes filled with treasure. Chocolate gold, as he thought of it. Because once word got around town that a new dealer was in the game—a dealer with connections and with the perfect, untraceable product that could be consumed anywhere, in public, in class, even at home under the most doting daddy's watchful eye—the masses had arrived on his doorstep.

Not literally, of course. He was careful to keep his identity well hidden, and made himself available only to the most trustworthy of those in the know. He made sure that whatever they had on him, he had twice on them. There was nothing on paper, nothing to connect him to the product, or the buyers, or to any illegal activity at all. Nothing except the candy bars themselves, chock full of illegal delights. And Kane kept those under lock and key.

This guy went by "KC" and dressed like a 90s rapper. Kane didn't care. He just cared about getting paid.

"It's all here?" he asked, when the envelope had changed hands.

"You don't have to count it, man," the guy said, hands shoved in his pockets and shoulders hunched. "You can trust me."

Kane sneered. "Right." He opened the envelope, leafed through the bills, did some quick mental math, then nodded. "Okay, you've got yourself a deal." He pulled a box out of his trunk. "Fifty bars. Should get you through the next week."

The idiot took the box and started to walk away without looking inside.

"Count them," Kane said. "I don't want you to start thinking you can trust me."

He counted—and, though Kane doubted the guy could make it past ten without using his toes, he counted all the way up to fifty, saluted, and then faded back into the night.

Kane stuffed the cash into his back pocket and got back into his car. Five hundred bucks. Not bad for a night's work. His phone rang again, just as he was about to start the car. Kane cursed. If the little twerp was trying to hit him up for more bars, or had some feeble complaint about the product—but then he glanced at the caller ID.

"Hey, babe," he said smoothly, bringing the phone to his ear. "You and Grace make it back without killing each other?"

"Barely," she said. "So . . . have a good night?"

He could hear it in her voice: She wanted to know. She was worried about where he'd been, what he was doing, why he wasn't with her. He couldn't blame her—but he also couldn't tell her. She'd never understand. And he refused to feel guilty about lying. That's who he was, and she'd known that from the beginning.

"Yeah, nothing big," he said. "Just had to do some stuff for my dad. You know how it is."

"Yeah," she said, in a voice that admitted no, she did not know how it was. "Well, I should probably go. I've to get some homework done for tomorrow."

"Two weeks to graduation and you're still doing homework? You're such a nerd."

"What's that make you?"

A nerd-lover, he was about to quip, but cut himself off just in time. Lovers, they were not. And *love* . . . it wasn't a word he wanted coming out of his mouth, in any form. "Just lucky, I guess."

"Nice save," she said dryly. "See you tomorrow?"

"I'll be the guy standing in front of your locker with a dozen red roses," he joked.

"I'd settle for some black coffee and a low-fat muffin."

"Split the difference?" he suggested. "How about a dozen carnations and a jelly doughnut?"

"'Night, Geary."

"Later, Stevens. Sorry I missed you tonight." And it was true, he thought as he hung up the phone. The wad of cash in his pocket felt good, and the evening had gone exactly as planned. But if he could have told Miranda the truth, if she could have been there to admire his work, and then to celebrate . . .

He cut himself off. He couldn't trust anyone with his secrets, not now. He couldn't afford to. And Miranda wouldn't get the beauty of his operation. She might try to stop him. Then he'd have to give up the business—or give up Miranda.

And he didn't see any reason why he should have to choose. He was Kane Geary, which meant he was used to having it all.

When he woke up, Fish and Hale were sitting a few feet away, staring. They looked unusually sober. Reed felt unusually tired and unusually sick—and he was pretty sure he was still a little drunk.

"What?"

"Dude, we need to talk," Fish said.

Reed's head hurt. He tried not to move it. "Talk about what?"

"About you."

"What is this, some kind of intervention?"

Hale glared at him. "This is serious, dude."

Reed snorted. That hurt his head too. "Like you've ever been serious."

"We're going on tour," Fish said. "After graduation."

"We talked it over," Hale said, "and we agreed."

"*We?*"

"Yeah, the band," Hale said.

"Since when does 'the band' not include me?" Reed asked.

"Since you stopped giving a shit," Fish snapped.

Reed sat up, despite the way it made his stomach lurch and the world spin. "Are you kidding me?" he asked. "Who's the one who always wants to rehearse? Who's the one who writes all the songs? And who's the one—ones—who sit around and get stoned all the time?"

"We're not kicking you out of the band," Fish said. "We're just telling you. We're going on tour after graduation. Three months, ten states. We'll sleep on the road. Hale's already got us a couple gigs."

"This was your idea, man," Hale said. "Remember?"

Reed remembered. He'd been stupid enough to think that they had a future—even though they never rehearsed, and they were always stoned and, more to the point, even though they sucked. It hadn't been his idea, not really. It had been Beth's. *Go on tour,* she'd urged him. *If you really want to make this thing happen,* work *at it. Get better. At least give it a try.* Beth was all about hard work. Except in her own life, apparently. Then she just wanted to take the easy way out.

Reed winced, and fumbled around in his pocket for another joint. But he was all out.

"What's the point of a tour?" he asked. "We suck. We're always gonna suck. Just let it go."

"And stay here for the rest of our lives?" Hale asked. "I'd rather die."

"There's stuff out there," Fish said. "There's *girls* out there. And we're going. Get your shit together and come with us."

"Or what?" Reed asked.

"Or stay here, and we'll get a new singer." Fish stood up and, a beat later, Hale did too. "She's not worth it, dude. She's just a girl."

Reed didn't know if he was talking about Beth or Kaia. Fish probably didn't know either.

"It's not about a girl," he said. "It's . . ." But he didn't know. It was buried, and he was too tired to dig for it.

Maybe it *was* just about a girl. But what did that mean? That he should forget her? That he should move on? That he should take her back?

She doesn't want to come back, he reminded himself. *She's back with her ex.*

Beth was the one who'd moved on. Beth, who should have stayed miserable and alone forever after what she'd done to him—and what she'd done to Kaia—had moved on. And Reed couldn't hate her for it. He couldn't hate her for any of it.

"So you're really going on tour?" he asked, lying back down on the couch.

"*We're* going," Fish said. "You know you want to get the hell out of this town."

Get the hell out. It sounded good. It sounded *right.* Reed took a deep breath, filling his lungs to capacity. It felt like the first deep breath he'd taken in a long time. His foggy head began to clear. Maybe he could do it. Clean up his shit. Figure out what to fix, what to forgive, and what to forget. Mind clear, soul free, he could start moving again. Get off the couch and off the booze. And get the hell out of town.

chapter

6

"Gutterball!" someone shouted gleefully in the background. But halfway down the lane, the ball veered away from the gutter and smashed into the cluster of pins. One after another tipped and wobbled, finally clattering to the ground. But two held their ground, separated by too much empty space.

"Shit," Kane muttered, collapsing onto the bench while he waited for the ball to return.

Miranda was waiting for him, her expression quizzical. "You okay?" she whispered.

Kane grunted. "I'm wearing shoes that probably have some other guy's toe mold growing on them, wasting a night with"—he glanced over his shoulder, where several of the guys from the basketball team were building a precarious tower of empty beer cans—"the goon squad. And now I've got to pick up an impossible spare. So yeah, I'm fine."

Miranda gave his upper arm a gentle squeeze. "That's not what I meant."

Kane shrugged her off. "I'm up," he said, reaching for his ball.

He lined himself up, took a few practice swings and, in his mind, mapped out the path the ball would need to take. Then he was ready. Arm drawn back, three loping steps, arm swinging forward, swift and smooth. Release. The ball flew from his fingertips, cracked against the wood, skidded down the varnished lane—and sailed through the empty space between the two pins.

This time, Kane didn't curse. He couldn't pretend to care about bowling, of all things. Not that night. He just fell back onto the bench and gave Miranda a wry grin. "Not my night, I guess."

She looked like she wanted to say something, and he steeled himself. That was the thing about girls. Always wanting to talk. Especially if they spotted a weakness, some chink in the armor. That's how it started: They slipped a finger through and widened the hole, just a bit, then a bit more, until, if you weren't careful, they eroded the protective covering entirely, and there you stood before them, naked.

And not in the fun way.

But Miranda didn't say anything. She just leaned against him and put her head on his shoulder.

Kane spent the next hour trying to decide whether to make up an excuse and ditch out on the night. He hadn't wanted to come in the first place, and under normal circumstances, he never would have agreed to it. A night of bowling with "the guys"—and their simpering girlfriends, half of whom Kane had gotten to first. It was a perfect storm of shit, but it was also the path of least resistance. And on this particular night, he didn't have the energy to resist.

As the boys broke for nachos, Miranda once again tipped her head toward his. "Want to get out of here?" she murmured.

They were in the parking lot before the guacamole was gone.

"Sorry about crapfest," Kane said, once they'd reached his car.

Miranda shrugged. "I told you before, I *like* bowling. Much as I suck."

"So why'd you want to leave?"

"You just looked . . ."

Kane tensed.

"Like you didn't want to be there," Miranda finally said.

Kane hunched over the steering wheel, his fingers gripping the ignition key. He didn't look at her. "Why'd you ask me that before? If I was okay?"

Miranda's hand fell lightly on his shoulder. "I know something's wrong," she said. "But you don't have to tell me."

Kane swallowed hard. Was he losing his touch? He'd filled the night with the requisite number of shrugs and smirks, burying his mood in the standard assortment of casual quips. No one should have been able to guess. No one else *would* have been able to guess.

Certainly another girl wouldn't have seen through the act. But another girl—at least the kind he was used to—wouldn't have known him so well. Or at all.

"I'm going to drive you home," he said abruptly. Her hand stayed on his shoulder.

"Okay."

They drove in silence. Miranda didn't ask why they were cutting the night short, and Kane realized he almost wanted her to. He tested a response in his head:

It was my mother's birthday yesterday. My father forgot. My brother forgot.

Which left me alone to celebrate. Just me and that ugly green vase on the fireplace where we keep her ashes.

I skipped the cake.

Kane would have laughed if it weren't so pathetic. He just couldn't say it out loud, even if he'd wanted to. The type of girl he was used to would listen to his sob story with tears in her eyes, and reward his sensitivity with a shower of kisses. But that type of girl would never hear this story. No one would.

Kane couldn't stand to be around other people, not when he was feeling like this.

But he made a sharp U-turn. "Let's go to my place."

Miranda looked at him in surprise. They almost never went to his place. "Sure."

What are you doing? he thought. Better to get rid of her, and sooner rather than later, before he said something stupid, something he would regret later. That would be the smart move.

But he didn't want her to go.

They ended up in his bedroom. Kane sprawled on the bed, flat on his back. Miranda curled up next to him, her arm thrown across his chest. The night before, he'd lain there alone, a half-empty bottle of scotch on his nightstand, the stereo blasting at full volume. This was better.

They didn't talk.

They always talked—it's what they did best. They bantered and sparred until Kane lost his train of thought staring at the pink flush rising in Miranda's cheeks and he stopped her latest rant with a kiss. She didn't let him get away with anything; except that night, she let him get away with shutting up.

"You remember in first grade, how we got to bring in cupcakes or something for the class on our birthdays?" he asked suddenly.

Miranda nodded, her chin digging into his shoulder.

"When it was my turn, my mother sent me in with a big box of strawberry cupcakes," he said. "Can you believe that? Freaking *strawberry*. What kind of first grader eats strawberry frosting?"

Miranda knew what had happened to his mother. She had to know, because she'd known him since they were toddlers—she'd been there. But he never talked about his mother, not to anyone. And Miranda knew that too. But she didn't mention it.

"I like strawberry frosting," she said quietly.

"That would make you the only one." Kane barked out a laugh. "Nobody wanted to eat them. The teacher had to send them all home with me at the end of the day. I could've killed her, you know? My mother. It was so stupid. *Strawberry.* I threw them all on the floor or something and locked myself in my room. I was such a little shit."

"Geary, you were six," Miranda pointed out. "That's what six-year-olds do."

"She never yelled at me," Kane said. "She never said anything about it, and never told my dad. When I finally came back downstairs, the kitchen was clean and there was a birthday cake waiting for me. Chocolate frosting."

Miranda propped herself up on an elbow and looked at him closely. Kane readied himself for a nauseating out-pouring of sympathy. It would be his own stupid fault.

She smiled. And then she kissed him, once, softly. "You were six," she said again. "And from what I remember, you were a spoiled brat. But it was your birthday . . . and she was your mom."

Kane shut his eyes for a second and closed his arms around Miranda. He wanted her there, he realized. It wasn't just that he didn't want to be alone or was too lazy to make up an excuse to get rid of her; it wasn't that she was a decently hot girl willing to climb into bed with him. It was *Miranda*, and he didn't want her to go.

That should have concerned him. There was a slippery slope between wanting and needing, and his sledding days were far behind him. The alarm bells should have been ringing. But they were silent.

He shifted onto his side, leaned in, and kissed her. She sighed as he pulled her toward him, their tongues tangled, their bodies twined.

"Feeling better?" she asked, a hint of a laugh in her voice, when they finally broke apart.

Kane raised an eyebrow, and this time he wasn't faking the smile. "So far, so good," he said, lunging for her again. "But definitely still room for improvement."

They'd been at it for an hour or so when the phone rang. Kane let go immediately and sat up, grabbing for his cell. "Sorry," he mouthed, "I have to . . ." Miranda shrugged, waiting quietly as he hunched over the phone

Finally, Kane snapped the phone shut and gave Miranda an apologetic look. "You're going to hate me, but . . ."

"Don't say it."

"I've got to take off." He leaned in to give her a quick peck on the lips, but she twisted away. Maybe it wasn't fair to be mad, not when he was obviously having such a crappy day, but it also wasn't fair for him to leave like this, abruptly and without explanation, *again*. She'd forced herself all night not to ask him what was wrong, even though it was obvious something was. And that had been the right choice. But how many things was she supposed to leave unspoken?

"How about Saturday," he suggested as they walked out to the car. "We can spend the day together and finish what we started. . . ."

"We've got Harper's graduation party on Saturday," Miranda reminded him.

Kane groaned. "That's not a *party*, it's some kind of PTA-approved freak show."

"Then it's too bad you promised to go, isn't it," she said, climbing into the passenger seat. He sighed and got in next to her.

"You're mad."

She shook her head. "Just drop me off and go wherever it is you're going." Kane's Camaro was in the shop, and Miranda had offered him her Civic for the week—but that was before she knew he was going to ditch her yet again and head out for . . . wherever it was he went after he got rid of her.

"Look, I'm *sorry*, but I've really got to—"

"It's fine," she said. If he could keep his moods to him-self, she could do the same. "Whatever. Let's just go."

"So now you're going to sulk?"

"I'm not sulking."

He darted a hand out and began tickling her, running his fingers lightly along her neck. She shivered and bit her lip to suppress the giggles, then smacked his hand away.

"Definitely sulking," he concluded. "I'll make it up to you, okay? Tomorrow night we'll—"

"I'm not *sulking*," she snapped. *Now or never,* she told herself. Miranda's first priority was to protect herself, and that meant getting the truth, whatever it was, on her own terms. Which meant *now.* "Where are you going, Kane?"

"It's private," he said, pulling the car out of the lot and turning onto the road that would lead them back to Grace.

"So private, you can't tell me?" she pressed.

"I'm supposed to tell you every little detail of my life? I didn't realize that was how this was going to work."

"It's not going to work at all if you keep ditching me to sneak off with some other girl." Miranda sucked in a sharp breath and pressed her hands to her lips. She hadn't been meaning to go that far.

Kane turned to look at her. "Is that really what you think?"

Fiery red with embarrassment, she stared straight ahead. "Can you just watch the road?"

Instead, he pulled over to the shoulder and turned the car off. "Stevens, look at me. Is that what you think I'm doing?"

Miranda shrugged. Think and fear were two different

things. But it was a yes on both fronts. What else could it be? "I don't know," she mumbled. "Maybe."

"Well, it's not."

She couldn't help herself. She snorted.

"What?" he asked.

"Of course that's what you'd *say*." She gave him a wry smile. "It doesn't mean you're not doing it."

"Stevens . . ." He brushed her hair away from her face and ran his fingers lightly across her lips.

"There's no other girl," he said firmly.

"Then what?"

"I can't tell you. You wouldn't approve."

"Why? Because I'm so naïve and uptight?"

His hands began crawling across her again, this time working their way up her thigh. "You weren't so uptight a few minutes ago. . . ."

"Kane!"

"Fine, fine, your loss." He took his hands away and, giving her a pointed look, placed them firmly on the steering wheel at ten and two o'clock, just like a good boy. "Better?"

Not exactly. But she nodded, anyway.

"It's just not your kind of thing, okay?" he said wearily. "You're going to have to trust me."

"They say every good relationship's built on a foundation of trust," Miranda mused.

"My point exactly."

"So . . ."

"So . . ." he echoed, when she didn't speak.

"So take me with you," she said firmly.

"What about trust?"

"Earn it." Miranda grinned defiantly and, reaching for

the steering wheel, rested her hand over his. "And maybe you'll find out you don't know me as well as you think."

Kane's eyes darted toward his watch, and he sighed. "Fine. You want to go, we'll go. But don't say I didn't warn you."

"Geary, everything about you says 'Danger, stay away,'" Miranda said as he laced his fingers with hers. "If I listened to warnings, don't you think I would have started with that one?"

Kane squeezed her hand and brought it to his lips. "It's not too late."

"Perfect," Beth muttered, giving the side of the car a sharp kick. "Just perfect." Not like it was a surprise: It had only been a matter of time before her parents' ancient Volvo gave up the fight. If the noisy clunking of the engine hadn't given that away, the goopy liquid dripping out of the exhaust pipe and the smoke that occasionally rose from the hood would have offered a substantial clue. Beth had just hoped it would happen when she wasn't driving.

But things didn't usually work out like that—as in, for the best. So she was the one behind the wheel when the car puttered to a stop, warning signs flashing, smoke pouring out of the hood, and the engine mercifully shutting down before it exploded, or whatever cars did when they'd reached their final resting place. Which, in this case, was the parking lot behind Guido's. She was tired, she was filthy, and all she wanted to do was get home in time to take a long bath before Adam picked her up for . . . well, it wasn't a date. Not quite, at least. But that didn't mean she wanted to reek of garlic and onions when he arrived at the house.

Beth called information to get the number for a tow truck. After putting her on hold for ten minutes, the man at the garage told her it could take two hours for someone to arrive.

"You can't come any faster?" she asked.

The guy on the other end of the phone grunted. "Got one driver out on a job, and the other's not in yet. He'll get there." And then, before she could say anything else, he hung up. So Beth waited in the parking lot—a safe distance from her car, in case it decided to explode after all—and hoped someone she knew would show up for a slice of pizza and offer to fix her car or at least give her a ride home.

Be careful what you wish for, Beth's father, the platitude king, liked to say.

The mud-spattered pickup pulled into the lot and parked just a few feet from her. There was nowhere to hide.

"Trouble?" Reed asked, leaning out the window.

A line from an old movie floated through her head. *Of all the pizza joints in all the towns in all the world, he walks into mine.*

Beth shook her head. "I'm fine."

He got out of the truck and walked past her and into Guido's. She considered her options. There was run—but to where? And then there was hide—immature, which wasn't a problem, but also unfeasible, which was. There was nowhere to hide, except in her car, which seemed both uncomfortable and unsafe. Especially given that more smoke was pouring out of it than ever. She supposed she could just start walking home—but what if, by some miracle, the tow truck actually arrived early? If she wasn't there to greet it, the guy would drive away again, leaving her sad little Volvo to rot.

So when Reed came out of the pizza place, she was still standing there, trying to decide what to do.

Reed walked past her again without pausing, without even glancing in her direction. He opened the door to the truck and got in, and only then did Beth realize she'd been holding her breath. The engine rumbled, and the truck sped toward the parking lot exit—then screeched to a stop.

He leaned out the window. "Get in."

"What?"

"You're stuck," he said. "Get in."

Beth tucked her hair behind her ears and tried to smile. "I'm fine. The tow truck is coming soon, and I have to wait around for it, so . . ."

"And who's gonna be driving the truck?"

"How am I supposed to—oh." His father worked there, she remembered. And Reed filled in for the drivers sometimes, to pick up extra cash.

"You're stuck with me either way," he said. "Get in, I'll drop you, then go back for the car."

Defeated, Beth crossed to the passenger side and, climbing in, breathed in the familiar aroma of leather and motor oil. "Thanks."

He didn't answer, just shifted into drive and pulled out of the lot. The radio was on, but she couldn't hear the music over the thunder of the engine. For several minutes they drove in silence. *This isn't so bad,* she thought. It was hard; it was painful, sitting there so close to him, knowing she had no right to ask him anything, to know how he was doing or how he was feeling, much less to reach over and touch his hand. His fingers were caked in grime. It was painful, all right, but she could handle it. The ride wouldn't last forever.

"You switch your shift?" he asked suddenly.

"What?"

"You didn't used to work today."

"Oh. Right. After everything that happened, I just thought I should, um, stay away. From . . . you."

"You could have just quit," he pointed out.

"I need the money, and—"

"I didn't mean you should have," he said. "I didn't mean anything."

"Oh."

His hair was sticking straight up, like he'd just rolled out of bed. It was wildly curly and tangled, like if she stuck her hand into its nest, she might never get it out.

"Doesn't matter, anyway," he said. "I'm out of here in a week. The band's going on tour."

"Really?" She knew she sounded bright and chirpy— and that was good. She didn't want to let on how it made her feel, the thought of him leaving town. She didn't have the right to feel that way anymore. And really, what was the difference? Whether he was in Grace or across the country, he was still out of her life. For good. "That's so great!"

He shrugged. "Yeah, I might not go. I don't know."

"You have to go," she insisted. "The Blind Monkeys are nothing without you."

"Yeah. Maybe."

There was another awkward silence. This time, Beth broke first. "I'm sorry about the prom. I really didn't think you'd still want to go."

"It was stupid," he said. "I should have . . . called. Or something."

"Look, Adam and I, we're not—"

"None of my business," he said quickly.

"I know, but I feel like I should explain."

"I don't care!" he shouted.

She flinched.

"Sorry," he said. "Can we just let it go?"

Beth turned her face toward the window and squeezed her eyes shut, listening to the rumbling engine and wishing the ride would end.

"Beth . . . I gotta ask you something."

"Okay."

"You don't have to tell me." He rustled his hair, leaving it wilder than ever. "But I need to . . . I have to ask."

"Anything," she promised. She knew there was nothing she could tell him that would help, much less fix things, but she could tell him whatever he needed to know. She owed him that much.

"Did you hate her?"

"Who?" Beth asked, afraid she knew.

"Kaia. I just, I need to know."

Beth sighed and leaned her head back against the coarse, grimy seat. "I wish I could say no, but . . . yeah. I guess I did. I thought I did. But I swear, Reed, I never meant for it to happen."

"You keep saying that," he said harshly. "So what *did* you mean?"

"I don't understand."

"What the hell were you doing? Why would you spike Harper's drink? What did you think would happen?"

She took a deep, shuddering breath. Thinking about everything that happened was nearly impossible, even when she was lying in bed, curled up under her blankets and trying to fall asleep. Revisiting it here, with *him*? It was torture. But she would do it, because she had to.

It helped that he was watching the road. Beth knew she wouldn't be able to say what she was about to say with his wide, dark eyes watching her.

"I was with Adam," she began, because everything began with him. "We'd been together for almost two years, and things were . . . not perfect. But good, you know? Then Kaia showed up, and at first, everything was okay, but . . ."

Beth told him everything. The way Kaia had mocked her, torn her down—and Adam had just ignored it. The plot Harper, Kane, and Kaia had concocted to tear her and Adam apart. The pain of hearing that Adam had lost his virginity to Kaia—had slept with her while he and Beth were still together, supposedly in love. And the glee on Kaia's face when she spilled the secret, ruining Beth's life with a few words and an icy smile.

"I just wanted to win," Beth admitted. "For once, I didn't want to be the one who played by the rules and got screwed. I wanted . . . I wanted her to know how I felt. I wanted . . ." She shook her head. "I don't even know. I don't know what I thought would happen. I didn't care. I just wanted her to *hurt*." Beth realized there were tears running down her face. This was the first time she'd said it out loud, and for a moment, she was back there. She felt the hate. "But I never thought she'd get in a car, or that Kaia . . . you've got to believe that," she pleaded. "I never meant for her to—" She forced herself to choke the word out. "Die."

And then she lost it. Beth pressed her hands against her face, trying to stop the tears, but they flooded out. She'd thought she was past the worst of it, but now it was all back and the wounds were just as fresh. Nothing had changed, she was still lost and alone, she was still a killer. Kaia was still dead. Her eyes filled with tears, her hands shielding her from the word, she couldn't see Reed, didn't know how he was reacting. She knew he didn't say anything to try to comfort her—and he didn't touch her.

She finally caught her breath, wiped her dripping nose on her sleeve, tried to rub the red out of her eyes, and then, finally, drawing her courage, dared to look up. The truck had stopped, and Reed was watching her. "Thanks."

Beth didn't trust herself to speak. She just nodded. They were parked in front of her house, and she realized he was just waiting for her to get out and leave him be.

She opened the door.

"I'll tow your car over to the shop," he said. "Someone'll call you and let you know the damage."

She nodded again. Then, forcing herself, said, "Thanks for making me come with you. You could have just left me there and—just, thanks for not abandoning me in the parking lot. For, you know, wanting to help."

For a moment, it looked like he was going to say something, but then the moment passed, and another, and then she got out of the truck and slammed the door, tears springing to her eyes again. She rubbed them away furiously.

"I wouldn't have left you there," Reed said. She whipped back around to face him through the open window, but he was staring in the other direction.

She waved, even though she knew he couldn't see her. And then he drove away.

They pulled up to a small barnyard, and Kane turned off the ignition. "Just remember," he warned Miranda. "You asked for this."

Miranda peered out the window at the dark, empty land surrounding them. "I think I can handle it."

He led her down a gravel walkway and over to a penned-in area. Three shadowy figures stood just outside the gate. When they got closer, she recognized them. Mark Walker and Jesse Lopez, two guys from the basketball team. And next to them, bending over and fiddling with something in the pen—

"Harper?" Miranda asked incredulously.

Harper whirled around. "You brought *her*?" she asked Kane.

Kane shrugged. "She said she wanted to come, so I figured."

"What's going on?" Miranda asked, looking back and forth from her boyfriend to her best friend to the guys who were unlocking the gate and leading something out on a leash, something that looked like . . . *a pig*?

Jesse Lopez handed the end of the leash to Kane, and Mark Walker led two more out of the pen, trying to hand one leash to Harper, who stepped back, holding up her hands in defense. "No way," she said quickly. "No way. I'm here in a supervisory capacity only. The pigs are *your* deal."

"What's going *on*?" Miranda asked again, louder this time. She glared at Kane. "You drove me all the way out here because you're . . . stealing pigs?"

"Not stealing," Kane said. "Borrowing. We have full permission of the owner."

Jesse raised a hand sheepishly. "It's my uncle," he explained. "I told him we'd have 'em back in a few days."

"And what are 'we' doing with them in the meantime?" Miranda asked, gaping as the fattest of the pigs began nibbling at Kane's shoelaces.

"You want to tell her?" Harper asked.

"Senior prank," Kane said, giving her a boyish grin. "We're keeping them in my yard for a couple nights, then when the time is right . . ."

"We set 'em off in school," Mark said, nearly salivating in anticipation. "And that's not even the best part."

Miranda cocked her head and turned to Kane, who was certain to be the one responsible. "And what, exactly, is the best part?"

"We draw numbers on them," Kane said proudly. "Piggie numbers one, two, and four."

"Where's number three?"

"That's the beauty of it," Harper explained. "It'll take them long enough to catch the first three pigs. Imagine how much time they'll waste looking for the fourth one—the one that doesn't exist!"

Miranda burst into laughter. "This is the dumbest thing I've ever heard."

"Welcome to the wonderful world of senior pranking," Harper said wryly. "It's a dirty job, but someone's got to do it." And, as Miranda knew, that someone was traditionally an elite group of seniors, handpicked by the previous senior class for their cunning, deviousness, ruthlessness and, most important, their cool factor. She should have realized that Harper and Kane would be at the top of the list.

"So what are we waiting for?" Miranda asked, taking one of the pig leashes out of Mark's hands. "Let's get these oinkers on the road!"

They led their livestock back into the darkness and, with some coaxing and—in the case of the largest pig—a fair amount of pushing, grunting, dragging, and cursing, got the pigs safely loaded into the back of Mark's pickup truck. As the others were securing the pigs, Kane pulled Miranda aside into the darkness.

"It's supposed to be a secret," he whispered. "That's why we didn't tell you. Plus, I didn't want to drag you down in the mud with me."

"I'm glad you did," she said, rising on her toes and giving him a quick kiss on the cheek. "If you're going to wallow in the mud"—she glanced down at her hands, which were streaked with grime—"why do it alone?"

"You never cease to surprise me, Stevens," he marveled.

"And you never cease to underestimate me, Geary," she said, slugging him on the shoulder. He grabbed her arm and spun her around so her back was pressed against his chest, wrapping his arms around her waist and resting his chin lightly on her head. She was a perfect fit. "When are you going to figure out that you can trust me?"

"You're not the one I'm worried about," he said softly.

Miranda turned around to face him and buried her head in his chest. His arms tightened around her, and she closed her eyes, savoring the moment.

She didn't ask what he'd meant.

"So tell me again why you can't interview me, Ms. Professional Journalist?" Adam demanded. He was sitting on the floor of his bedroom, his back against the bureau and his feet kicked up against the wall. Beth was straddling the desk chair.

Both of them had, without mentioning it, avoided the bed.

"Conflict of interest," Beth said. "And I'm not a professional journalist. Not yet. If I screw up this story . . ."

"You won't screw it up," he said firmly. He'd been saying it all night.

Six months ago, it wouldn't have been like this. Beth would have thrown herself into the new project with determination and surety, vowing to impress the newspaper staff so much, they offered her a job on the spot. Adam didn't have to wonder what had happened to that Beth. He knew.

She stood up and walked over to the window, which faced the backyard. It also faced Harper's bedroom, which was why, these days, he usually kept the blinds down.

"Adam, I need to—" She stopped, her back to him.

"What is it?" he asked, when she didn't continue.

But she just shook her head. "Nothing." She'd been doing it all night, starting to say something, then cutting herself off in the middle as if she'd lost her nerve. Or maybe he was just projecting, because he'd been doing the same thing. The UC-Riverside coach had called again today, checking in on his progress, wondering if he'd made a decision yet. He hadn't. And, much as he would have liked to talk it over with Beth—the *old* Beth—he knew this one couldn't help him. She probably couldn't handle hearing about it in the first place. So he kept his mouth shut.

"You've been really great tonight," she said. "Thanks for taking me out."

"We had to celebrate!" he said. "This is huge."

"Yeah. Maybe." She turned back to face him. "Do you want to go outside for a while? Sit on the rock and . . . talk?"

"No," he said, too quickly.

She blanched, and turned quickly back to the window. "Oh. Of course not. I should probably just get out of here. I'm sure you've got stuff to do, and . . ."

"No. It's not that."

Adam saw her shoulders heave with a deep, shuddery breath, then another. He stood up and crossed the room to join her at the window. The light in Harper's bedroom was on; he suppressed the urge to close his blinds. What were the odds that she was watching? He tilted his head, leaning it against Beth's. "It's not that," he said. "I just . . . I don't want to go outside, okay?"

He couldn't take Beth out there to the rock, to his and Harper's place, the long, flat rock that lay on the boundary between their properties, where they'd spent so many hours of their lives lying side by side talking about everything that strayed across their minds. Where they'd shared their first kiss, complete with awkward fumbling and entangled braces—and where, this year, they'd shared far more than that. Even if Harper never spoke to him again, that place would still belong to the two of them.

Adam turned slightly, and so did Beth, until they were facing each other. He watched her eyes, pale blue and glittery, like a pool of water at dawn; she didn't look away. He didn't know who leaned in first. It just happened. One moment they were standing apart, their arms resting on the windowsill, lightly touching, Beth's lips, covered in pink gloss, slightly parted and curling up in a half smile. The next moment, they were kissing. Adam had time to think about the silhouette their faces would make in the window, shadowy lips connected, shadowy hands pressed against shadowy faces—if anyone was watching. And then Beth pushed him away.

"I'm sorry," he said, confused. "Did I . . . ?"

"No. I shouldn't have." She stepped away.

"I thought it was what you wanted," he said helplessly.

"You thought . . ." She sighed, and slid down the wall into a sitting position, curling her legs up against her chest. "I heard you. A couple days ago in the parking lot. With Kane."

"What are you talking about?" Adam slumped down next to her—keeping a few inches of space between them.

"I know you're only hanging out with me because you feel sorry for me," she said, her voice thin and flat.

"I don't know what you think you heard, but—"

"Please, Adam. Just . . . I heard you." She turned to look at him, and she wasn't crying. Her lips weren't trembling, nor was her voice. "Can't you just admit it?"

"Fine." He hated this. Hated everything about it. "I guess I feel kind of sorry for you. But that's not all of it."

"I know." She sighed heavily. "You think you owe me. I heard that, too. And I guess . . . I already knew. It's the way you look at me. Like you think I'm going to break or something. You're scared of what will happen if you walk away. I knew that. I just . . . I didn't want to know. You know?"

He couldn't deny it.

"You'd rather be with Harper," she said. "And you should be."

Adam shook his head. "That's not going to happen."

"Only because you're with me," Beth said. She touched his arm, lightly, and then dropped her hand back onto her knees. "Because you think I'll fall apart if you're not here. But that shouldn't have to be your problem."

She was giving him an out. And he was tempted to take it. But. There was always a but.

"But it's true, right? What happens if I ditch you, like everyone else?"

She sniffled, and looked down. "I'd be fine."

"Now who's lying?"

"I don't want to need you," she said in a choked, angry voice. "I don't want to be that girl, some weak, broken thing dragging you down."

"You're not," he assured her.

"I should be stronger than that."

"You will be," he promised. "But for now . . ."

"Yeah. For now." She pressed her hand to her mouth and made some noise that could have been a laugh or a sob. "So here we are."

Adam scooted over a couple inches and looped his arm around her shoulders, pulling her toward him. She didn't resist. He tugged her closer, and she laid her head against his shoulder while he stroked her arm, gently, rhythmically, up and down, up and down. "Here we are," he echoed. And they sat like that for a long time, eyes closed, bodies together, without moving, until Beth felt strong enough to go home.

chapter

7

The conversation went like this.

Harper: "No. There's no way. Just *no*."

Amanda Grace, Harper's ever-doting mother, torch-carrier for the Grace family heritage, and president of the Haven High PTA: "I'm not asking you, I'm telling you."

Harper, her arms folded: "Then I'm not coming."

Richard Grace, without looking up from his newspaper: "You're coming."

Harper: "Is it your goal in life to humiliate me?"

Amanda Grace: "I'm not asking you to stand on the roof and sing the national anthem. I'm just asking you to be there."

Harper: "And to smile, and make nice, and pretend I don't hate every single person there."

Amanda Grace: "Yes, that, too."

Harper had stormed up the stairs, defeated. And then she had managed to put the whole thing out of her mind. Until the invitations arrived. As if things weren't bad enough already. The invitations were made from a thick card stock, dyed pale blue and dotted with tiny green and lavender flowers. *Con-GRAD-ulations!* they announced, in tacky pink letters. The "o"s had been turned into balloons.

Amanda Grace was displeased. She had requested something tasteful, but the result was half bridal shower, half kiddie birthday party, and all awful. She sent them out, anyway. And then *Harper* was displeased. Because her mother sent them out to everyone. Every single person in the senior class. Including Lester Lawrence—or Lawrence Lester, Harper could never remember which it was—who would probably bring his pet crickets. Including Ellen Blumenthal and Margaret Cheever, who still worshipped the Powerpuff Girls. Including the ditzy cheerleaders and the boneheaded jocks and the math club losers and all the guys she'd ever hooked up with and all their former and current and jealous girlfriends.

Including Adam.

"It doesn't matter if you don't like them. This party isn't for you," her mother reminded her as Harper stood at the edge of the kitchen, waiting to make her grand entrance into the backyard where the detestable masses had invaded her only remaining sanctum. She was wearing a black slipdress with a red sash and a plunging neckline that her mother complained was too dressy and too dark for the occasion. Harper didn't care; she felt dark. And she figured she might as well look hot.

Her mother handed her a bowl of cheese curls. "This party is for your class. It's a celebration." There was steel in her voice. "So *smile.*"

Harper smiled, prepared herself, and stepped outside.

"Hey, Harper, your house is so great!" burbled some girl who, under normal circumstances, Harper would pretend didn't exist. She smiled and elected not to comment on the neon monstrosity the girl was wearing as a dress.

"Awesome party," some loser surf-talked, giving her a "hang ten" wave as if the nearest ocean weren't hundreds of miles away. Harper ducked her head, dropped the cheese curls on a nearby table, and barreled across the yard toward Miranda and Kane. The happy couple looked disgustingly content in their little corner, playing with each other's hair, gazing into each other's eyes, and pretending the rest of the world didn't exist. It was gross, but it was better than nothing.

"Thanks for coming," she muttered, taking a quick swig from Kane's ever-present flask.

"Rockin' party," Kane said sarcastically, nodding toward the pastel streamers Amanda Grace had hung from the trees and the old speakers that were pumping out some kind of 90s hip-hop in a feeble attempt to seem hip.

Harper sighed. "It's a good thing high school's ending in a week, because I'd never live this one down."

"Look on the bright side," Miranda pointed out. "No one whose opinion you care about is dumb enough to show up." Harper had done an efficient job of spreading the word that the event would be about as thrilling as a PTA bake-off, and suggested that her fellow A-listers hold out for Savannah Miller's party a few nights later. Savannah was a drab nobody who'd barely registered on Harper's radar since seventh grade, when the two of them had been stuck together for a history project and Savannah had irritatingly refused to cheat. But she was rich, and her parents

were out of town, which—thanks to Harper's help—
opened the possibilities for true greatness. Let Amanda
Grace have her garden party; Harper would have a raging
night to remember. Even if she had to have it at someone
else's house.

"Yeah, that's the good news," Harper said. "The bad
news is that every single loser showed, and now we're stuck
with them."

"*You're* stuck with them," Kane corrected her. "We're
putting in our face-time, and then"—he tapped his watch
and winked—"it's time for some oink-oink."

"I never thought I'd say this," Harper said, "but I'd
rather be wrestling pigs in the high school gym than here
stuffing my face with cheese puffs and pretending these
people don't make me sick."

"Don't worry, Grace," Kane said kindly. "Every time we
look at those pigs, we'll be thinking of you."

"You're such a sweetheart." Harper looked over his
shoulder, scanning the faces in the pathetic crowd.

"He's not here," Miranda said quietly.

Harper turned back around. "What are you talking
about?" But she couldn't fool Miranda.

"It's still early," Miranda said hopefully. "Maybe . . ."

Harper shook her head. "It doesn't matter. Let's snag
some of those mini-quesadillas before they're all gone,
okay?"

And Miranda, thankfully, let it drop.

Harper managed to keep up a steady stream of chatter
for the next two hours, standing at the fringes with
Miranda and Kane, picking apart the wardrobes and per-
sonalities of their fellow seniors as Harper pretended she

wasn't keeping one eye fixed on the gate, waiting for Adam to walk through it. But then Miranda and Kane left, and it was a lot harder for her to pretend she wasn't miserable.

The later it got, the harder it was for her to convince herself that he might still show. People were starting to leave, and the only new arrivals in the last hour had been—

"No." Harper gaped at the entry gate. "Oh, no, I don't think so." She stormed across the yard and planted herself in front of them, hands on hips, fierce scowl on her face. There was nothing she could do about her mother, and there was nothing she could do about Adam, but *this* was a problem she could handle.

"What are *you* doing here?" she asked in disgust, staring down her two sophomore clones: pathetic, brainless twits who dressed like her, talked like her, and wouldn't leave her alone. In the beginning she'd been flattered—after all, you couldn't fault their taste. But the monkey-see, monkey-do act had gotten old a long time ago. "This is a *senior* party."

"We know!" the one on the left said, nearly clapping her hands with excitement. She'd dyed her hair since Harper had seen her last, and her curls were now the exact shade of brown with reddish streaks that Harper saw in the mirror every morning. Harper's nickname for her—Mini-me—had never seemed so apt.

"We can't believe it!" That would be Mini-she, the best friend, whose arm was covered in the same thin jelly bracelets Harper had worn for a few weeks back in May before getting sick of the look. "It's so sad that you're graduating," she moaned. "We're going to miss you sooooooo much."

"I said, what are you doing here?" Harper asked again, knowing she would have to get them out before her mother spotted them. In Amanda Grace's book there was only one thing tackier than crashing a party: making a scene by tossing out the crashers.

"Do you mind?" Mini-me asked. "We just wanted to come and tell you how much we're going to miss you next year."

"Soooooooo much," Mini-she added, sounding even more cowlike than she had the first time.

It was perfect, Harper thought. A symbol of the disaster her life had become: her two clingy, sycophantic clones crashing the lame excuse for a party that Harper would have done anything to escape, while the only person she had really wanted to be there never bothered to show up. Suddenly, she was fed up—with her oppressive mother, with the losers invading her backyard, with the pride that wouldn't let her make things right with Adam, and, most of all, with the Minis, these girls who had plagued her all year long, who wouldn't give her a moment of peace. *Enough,* she thought. *This is finally enough.*

"Get out," she said coldly. "You're not welcome here."

"But Harper," Mini-me whined, "I know we're not seniors, but we thought since we were your friends—"

"My *friends*?" she sneered. "You think I'd ever be friends with someone like you? Someone who can't even come up with her own identity, so you have to steal mine?" She started to laugh. "You're not even *good* at it." She pointed at Mini-she's hideous floral miniskirt. "I wouldn't wear that rag to take the trash out. I wouldn't even *use* it as a rag to wipe the bathroom floor."

Mini-she's lip wobbled, and Mini-me took a step backward, her eyes wide. "We just wanted to . . ."

"Wanted to what?" Harper asked. They didn't answer. "Wanted to *what*? No, I didn't think you'd come up with anything, because you don't want anything—how could you? You're nobody. You're clones. You're cheap knock-offs. You only want what you think *I* want." She shook her head, as if in pity, though she felt none. "I'd tell you to get lives of your own, but somehow, I just don't think you can handle it. But here's an idea: If you've got to steal someone's life, make it someone other than me. You got that?"

The girls were frozen, unwilling to speak but afraid to look away.

"I said, *You got that*?" Harper repeated angrily. "Get out of my face and find someone else to copy. I can't deal with it anymore. It's too pathetic. You're too pathetic."

If they'd gotten angry, she might have felt guilty. She might even have apologized. If they had yelled back, or even rolled their eyes and turned silently, walking out with their chins up and their shoulders back, Harper might have realized that she'd misjudged them. She might have reminded herself that even though they acted like mindless clones, they *did* want something: her friendship. She might have felt the way she had at the beginning of the year: sympathetic. Flattered. Even—if they had shown the slightest hint of rebellion or self-preservation or dignity—a little impressed.

But they didn't. Mini-me turned red. Mini-she stared at the ground. And then Mini-me actually said it. "I'm sorry." And they spun around and skittered away.

The adrenaline flooded out of her. She felt like shit. And she wished she could take it all back. Not because she felt guilty, or because she'd been cruel. But because Mini-me and Mini-she had worshipped her. They'd wanted to *be* her—which made them proof that she was someone worth being.

And now the proof was gone.

Heather Martinez, age 17, interview #1

Q: If you could do high school all over again, what would you do differently?

A: I'd never hook up with Rodney, that's number one. Asshole. Did you hear what he said about me to—

Q: I mean, in the broader sense. You know, if you could change what high school was like.

A: Oh. Yeah. Um, I guess maybe I wouldn'tve taken Spanish, because that French teacher guy was pretty hot, you know, before he disappeared. And I would've . . . well, maybe I would've studied a little, you know, actually gotten some decent grades so I wouldn't have to go work at my mom's store after graduation and I could actually get out of here, you know? Do something.

Q: What would you do?

(Interviewer note: Subject doesn't answer for several minutes.)

A: Maybe . . . this is gonna sound kind of stupid, but . . . maybe be a teacher?

Q: Why is that stupid?

A: You know. What kind of idiot comes back to school once they finally let you out? I always used to say that, after graduation, I'd never walk into a school again. And . . . yeah, I guess I won't.

Kyle Chuny, age 18, interview #4

A: I didn't think you knew who I was.

Q: We've gone to school together for fifteen years. Why wouldn't I?

A: I don't know. I guess . . . no one ever seems to know who I am. It's like all these kids that I used to hang out with in elementary school, now they blow past me in the hall like they don't even know me. I asked this girl out once, right? I knew she was going to say no, but I figured whatever, right? This was last year. So I asked her to the junior prom. And she just looked at me like I was crazy, and she was like, "Aren't you a sophomore?" Then she just started laughing. And when I told her I was a junior, she laughed even harder.

Q: Does it make you mad?

A: Whatever. It's just high school, right? And now it's over. And I figure in college, things'll be different in college. People will be different, you know?

Q: Why?

A: What do you mean? It's college. College people.

Q: Aren't college students just high school students one year older?

A: No, no way. It's like a whole different thing in college. Everything's different. It has to be.

Barbara Morris, age 18, interview #6

Q: Will you miss high school?

A: Yeah, of course I will. I'm totally psyched for college next year, but everyone here is so great. I'm never going to make friends like this again. I mean, I know everyone talks about how you meet all these great friends in college, but can they ever really know you? How can anyone really know you if they don't know where you came from? It's not like your friends from home—nothing will ever be like that.

Q: So you're going to keep in touch with them?

A: Yeah, we made a pact. We're going to e-mail every day, no exceptions. It's going to make it easier to leave—knowing that there's someone out there, s omeone who knows who you really are.

Q: Does that mean you're nervous about college next year?

A: No. Definitely not. I've been waiting for this my whole life. I've got it all planned out. I'm going to major in political science, write for the newspaper, then get into a good law school, make law review, and become a constitutional lawyer. Who knows, maybe I'll even make it to the Supreme Court.

Q: Sounds like you've got it all figured out.

A: It's not hard, when you know exactly what you want.

Ashley Statten looked up from the interview notes that Beth had carefully prepared for her. "What the hell is this?" she asked, throwing them down on her desk. "Is this some kind of joke?"

Beth shifted her weight from one foot to the other. Ashley hadn't offered her a chair. The newsroom was pretty dead—everyone else had headed home to enjoy their Saturday night, but Ashley was scrambling to meet her deadline and apparently wanted Beth to share in her misery. "If that's not exactly what you needed, I've got a lot more," Beth said. She'd spent hours the night before transcribing all her interviews and pulling out the moments that she thought were most revealing. Telling herself that this was the start to her journalism career. It was almost enough to assuage the sickening feeling she got listening to all these seniors talking brightly about the future. It seemed like everyone else was looking forward while Beth was still stuck in the past.

"More? Spare me." Ashley stood up and walked over to a metal filing cabinet against the side wall. She pulled a digital camera out of the cabinet and brought it over to the desk. "I knew this was a bad idea," she muttered. "What would someone like you know about *real* journalism?" She waved the camera at Beth, who took it in confusion. "You know how to use this thing?"

"Um, I guess so. But . . . use it for what?"

Ashley glared at her. "Look, another time, maybe, I'd sugarcoat this, but I don't have the time, so let me be blunt. These interviews suck. They're tepid, they're boring, they're totally off-topic. You let your subjects ramble. You don't press them on the hard questions. You don't get *anything* juicy out of them. To be honest, I just don't see much journalistic instinct here. And your subjects? Where are the alpha girls? Where's the head cheerleader? The star quarterback? The school slut? Where's my story?"

"I can do better," Beth said quickly.

"I doubt it," Ashley said. "But that's moot. I don't have enough time to send you back out there, and lucky for you, I've got most of the material I need from my own interviews. But here's the good news, for you, at least. My editor has a real hard-on for that English teacher of yours, and she thinks you're God's gift to journalism—which means that unless you burn the place down, you're probably going to get that internship next year. So here's all I need you to do. Take the camera. Hit a party—there's one coming up on Tuesday night."

"How do you know?"

"Because *I* actually did some investigative reporting," Ashley said. "Maybe you've heard of it? Look, I'd go myself, but"—she gestured down at her tailored gray suit—"obviously I'd have a little trouble blending. So it's on you. Take some pictures—and no more of this 'best times of our lives' crap. This story is about the dark side of high school, and I want you to get me some good-girls-gone-wild pics to go along with it. From what I hear about Haven parties, shouldn't be too tough. Think you can handle it?"

"We'll see." Ashley waved Beth away like a mosquito and turned back to her computer. "Do even a mediocre job and you'll get your precious internship, whether you deserve it or not. But, Beth?"

Beth paused on her way to the door, wondering if even a real journalism internship would be worth facing Ashley Statten day in and day out. "Yes?"

"Don't screw up again."

"I think number four belongs in the principal's office," Miranda said, holding steady as the pig jerked forward on its leash and squealed in frustration.

"And *I* think my girlfriend's a criminal mastermind," Kane said, trying to kiss her. She squirmed away.

"Not in front of the pig," she teased.

They crept down the dark hallway, the distant pitter-patter of little footsteps telling them that pigs number one and two were already well on their way to causing trouble. When they reached the central administration office, Kane brandished a key.

"Do I want to know where you got that from?" Miranda asked.

Kane shook his head. "Probably not."

He let them into the office, and they released the pig, slamming the door shut before it could escape. Miranda burst into nervous giggles—she still couldn't believe she was doing this: trespassing, smuggling livestock, defiling school property. It was so *not* her. But it was Kane, and she was pretty proud of herself for keeping up. With only a minimum of nervous questions and heart palpitations.

"You're sure there are no security cameras?" she asked as they slipped toward an exit.

"This is Haven High, not the Pentagon," Kane said. "Trust me, I've done this plenty of times."

"Why—no, never mind." She rolled her eyes. "I don't want to know."

"Again, probably not." Suddenly he froze, and grabbed her, raising a finger to his lips. Miranda's mouth formed a silent O of horror as she heard the footsteps. Not scuttling pig patters, but solid, heavy steps. Headed in their direction.

"Is there someone there?" a deep voice called out, and a weak flashlight beam broke through the darkness.

"Shit," Kane whispered.

Miranda was shaking. One week to graduation, and now . . . what would her mother say if she got thrown out of school?

Kane grabbed her arms and squeezed tight. "Calm down," he whispered. "We got this. When I say the word, just run for the exit. Fast as you can. Okay?"

Miranda shook her head. "We have to hide. Maybe . . ."

"No. Run," Kane mouthed. "Trust me?"

She nodded.

"What are you kids up to down there?" the security guard came into sight. "Hey, hey you—get out here!"

"Now!" Kane mouthed, and Miranda ran.

"What the—?" They slammed past the security guard before he could stop them and burst through the exit.

"Keep going!" Kane shouted, and Miranda sprinted across the field and down the hill to the parking lot, flinging herself into the passenger seat of her car while Kane leaped into the driver's seat and peeled out nearly before she'd managed to slam the door.

"Go!" she screamed. "Go!" She didn't breathe again until they were safely out on the main road, lost in the flow of Saturday night traffic. "You don't think he saw the car, do you?" she asked. "If he caught the license number . . ."

"Did you get a look at that guy?" Kane asked scornfully. "Probably burst an artery halfway out the door."

"Be nice," Miranda chided him, but it did make her feel better to think of the guard's potbelly and the way his footsteps had fallen behind them so quickly. They were safe. And they'd pulled it off.

Kane pulled into the empty lot of a shoe store that had closed hours before. He turned the car off.

"What are we stopping for?" Mirada asked.

"This." He turned to her, grabbed her face in both hands, and kissed her, hard and deep. "We did it."

"We really did, didn't we?" Adrenaline was shooting through her. Her hands were tingling, and she felt like her head was about to pop off. "I can't believe I did that. It was—we could have gotten in so much trouble, but . . ."

"It was worth it, wasn't it?" Kane asked, with a knowing grin.

"Totally. It was amazing." She touched his cheek, rubbing her fingers against his jawline. "*You're* amazing. I never would have . . . before. I just mean—this is incredible. Being with you. I've never been so happy, and sometimes I just think, it's like everything I've ever wanted is finally—" She cut herself off in horror.

Kane didn't say anything.

You scared him away, she thought furiously. *It was the perfect moment, and you ruined everything.*

"I didn't mean, I just meant, you know, we had a good night, and—" She was babbling, trying to fix it, but it couldn't be fixed. It was ruined. "You know, it's just cool, hanging out and all, and I'm just a little wired from the criminal activities and—"

"Come here," he said, drawing her into his arms. "I had fun too," he whispered, and kissed her again. Maybe he hadn't understood what she was saying. Maybe he had chosen to ignore it. Or maybe this was his way of saying that he agreed, that they *weren't* just having fun, that this was something more for him, too. Miranda didn't know. She just knew that she'd almost screwed everything up and yet he was still there, still real, kissing her, holding her and, even with her arm wedged against the glove compartment and the gearshift digging into her thigh, she was happier than she'd ever been.

She would just have to be more careful. She couldn't afford to risk telling him how she really felt, that she was falling in—

No, she couldn't even afford to *think* it. Not yet. She would just be patient, and maybe someday *he* would say it. And then she could let everything out and stop worrying that she would do something to make him leave. It hurt— the worrying and the waiting, always expecting that something awful was about to happen—but she was willing to give it time. She was willing to trust him. She just hoped she could trust herself to stay silent.

Kane could never find out that she was falling in love.

It's not too late, she thought, knocking on the door. *You can still run away.*

But then the door swung open.

"Oh, Harper!" Adam's mother leaned toward her to give her a hug. Harper could smell the whiskey on her breath. "So charmin' to see you." The slur in her words was so slight, it might not have been noticeable to someone who wasn't looking for it. But when it came to Adam's mother, Harper was always looking. "C'mon in."

"Actually, could you just let Adam know I'm here?" She didn't know why she didn't want to go in the house. It wasn't just Mrs. Morgan. The idea of being trapped in there with him . . . she couldn't do it. So she waited on the porch as Mrs. Morgan called her son downstairs.

"I'm juss having a lil' drink," Mrs. Morgan said in her heavy Southern accent. "Y'all sure you don't want to come in and have some?"

"I'm fine," Harper said. Adam's mother always made

her vaguely uncomfortable. Maybe because she had never been able to forget the day she'd walked into Adam's kitchen and discovered his mother lying on the kitchen table . . . with their seventh-grade math teacher lying on top of her.

"You kids have fun," Mrs. Morgan told her son when he finally arrived in the doorway. She pinched his cheeks, which he endured, as he always did. "Don't you do anything I wouldn't do." She was still cackling as they closed the door in her face.

Adam blushed. "You know my mom, she's just . . ."

"Yeah." Harper swallowed hard. "You didn't come."

"What?"

"To my party. You didn't come."

Adam looked like he didn't know what he was supposed to say. "I just figured you won't want me there."

"I don't get why you would—"

"Harper, you made it perfectly clear that you don't want me around."

"And you know why," Harper snapped.

"Yeah, I do. So unless you changed your mind . . ."

"You know I can't—"

"Fine." Adam turned and opened the screen door. "We can't keep having this same conversation."

She grabbed his arm. "Wait."

They paused like that, her fingers wrapped around his bicep. She missed the feel of him. "I don't want to fight." Harper didn't know why she couldn't stay away from this place. "Can we just . . . take a break from all that?" she asked finally. "Pretend like none of it matters, just for tonight?"

"Temporary truce?"

She nodded, and they shook on it.

"Backyard?" Adam asked, and headed around to the back before she could answer. He just knew what she wanted. He knew her.

They lay on their backs on the wide, flat rock, their arms splayed out and almost touching, but not quite. Harper had always loved lying next to someone, listening to their breathing, a silent confirmation that she wasn't alone. Adam's was slow and steady. She wished she could put a hand on his chest and feel its gentle rise and fall. "Remember when we built the fort?" she asked. They'd propped some cardboard and wooden planks against their rock, then pillaged the Grace family linen cabinet and strung up Amanda Grace's antique silk sheets as tarps.

"I thought you were going to be grounded forever," Adam said, chuckling.

"You would have rescued me," Harper reminded him. They had come up with a secret plan, involving a ladder, two skateboards, and enough supplies (candy bars and Gatorade) to last them several days "in the wild." Fortunately, the grounding had only lasted a week; they'd never had to run away.

"That's my specialty," Adam said. "Remember when we 'camped out'?"

Harper snorted. "I can't believe I let you talk me into that." In sixth grade, they had pitched a tent in the backyard. Adam told ghost stories, while Harper complained about the bugs. "So gross."

"And when that cricket climbed into your sleeping bag . . ."

"Ew!" Harper squealed, and jerked her limbs as if she

could still feel the insect skittering up her body. "Don't go there. I can't even *think* about that."

"Hey, I saved you, didn't I?"

She smiled, glad that it was too dark for him to see her face. "Yeah, I guess you did." He had gotten rid of the cricket, dried her tears, and talked her out of going inside. Then he'd promised to stay up all night, "guarding" her. It was the only way she'd been able to fall asleep.

"Things are really ending, aren't they?" she said. "I mean, high school, living at home, all that." But that's not what she meant, not completely.

"Yeah." He was quiet for a moment. "Next year . . . This place, it seems like nothing ever changes. But now . . ."

"Everything's changing." She turned over on her side and watched his face, silhouetted in the moonlight. It suddenly seemed so stupid, the way she'd pushed him away, just for trying to do the right thing, just for trying to protect someone else. He was Adam Morgan, that's what he did: protected. Rescued. Saved. It was why she loved him. So why couldn't she just get over it? Harper inched her hand across the cool surface of the boulder until her index finger brushed up against his wrist. She was so close. If she could just stop hating Beth so much, if she could just ignore that part of his life and accept that she didn't get to have *all* of him . . .

She moved her hand, feeling like she was pushing an enormous weight. Her muscles strained—her heart strained—and then it was done. Her hand rested on his, their fingers merged together. He didn't move. "Adam . . ."

"I might go away to college next year," he said suddenly.

She took her hand away.

"What?"

"A recruiter came. A basketball coach, from UC Riverside. He offered me a spot on the team, and a scholarship, and . . ."

Say congratulations, she told herself furiously. *Sound happy.* Be *happy.*

"UC-Riverside," she said instead, her voice thin and flat. "That's, like, hundreds of miles away."

"Yeah. It's a five-hour drive."

"So are you . . . when do you leave?"

Adam sat up and rubbed his hands across his face. "I don't know if I'm going yet. I haven't decided." He turned to her. "What do you think?"

Stay, Harper thought, wishing he could hear. *Stay for me.*

She shrugged. "Your call. It sounds really . . . great. For you."

"Maybe." And without warning, he reached for her hand. She let him take it, let him press it between his palms. A warm tingling rose up her arm. "Gracie, I don't want to leave with the way things are. . . ."

Leave. He was leaving.

She pulled her hand away and climbed off the rock. "I have to go home," she said without emotion. Every feeling she had was locked up tight, because if she let even one dribble out, the floodgates would open.

"Now?" Adam jumped off the rock as well and tried to take her hand again, but she stepped away.

"It's late. I should—I have to go."

"I'll walk you home," he said, sounding almost desperate.

"No." And she said it firmly enough that he didn't protest.

He was leaving her, she thought, as she waved good-bye and walked slowly through the darkness. She was in no hurry to get home; she just needed to get away. At least for tonight, she had to leave him first.

chapter

8

"You sure you want to do this?" Adam asked.

Beth took a deep breath and grabbed her camera. "Want to? No. But let's go."

They threaded through the crowd, Beth snapping pictures and feeling like a total loser.

"So whose house is this?" she asked as they stepped into the entry hall. It stank of beer.

Adam shrugged. "Who cares?"

"Yo, Morgan!" someone called, and it was echoed by shouts from all over the room. A few guys from the basketball team hurried to knock fists with him and boast about their keg stands.

"Hey, Adam." A cheerleader named Brianna draped herself around his neck. He pried her off. "Going to miss me next year?"

"Sure."

"Because I'm going to miss you," she whispered, almost crawling up his arm. "Want me to show you how much?"

"Not really." Adam shook her off and turned to Beth. "Sorry about, uh . . ."

She shook her head. "Don't worry about it." She wasn't jealous. At least, not in the normal way. But she couldn't help noticing the way everyone turned to look at Adam as he passed by, their faces lighting up when he smiled or waved. Everyone wanted to talk to him, to touch him, even just to be acknowledged by him. Beth, on the other hand, was invisible.

She snapped a couple more pictures, but she couldn't figure out where to point the camera. Whenever anyone caught sight of her, they froze and stuck on a pained smile. Something told her Ashley Statten wouldn't approve.

"Want a drink?" Adam asked, nodding at the keg. Beth shook her head. "Yeah, I probably shouldn't, either."

"I can drive home," Beth offered. But he just shrugged. He hadn't wanted to come in the first place, even though everyone claimed this would be the best graduation party in years. But Beth hadn't had the nerve to come alone.

A tall, dark-haired senior Beth didn't recognize approached them, slapping palms with Adam. "Yo, Morgan, haven't seen you since the season ended."

"Hey, Jake," Adam said, his first genuine smile of the night making an appearance. He turned to Beth. "This is Jake, he's a point guard for Crestview—almost beat us out for the championship this year."

"*Almost* being the operative word," Jake said ruefully. "And this would be?"

"This is Beth," Adam said, "my, uh . . ."

"Nice to meet you," Beth said quickly, shaking his hand.

"*The* Beth?" Jake raised his eyebrows. "Nice to meet you, too." He tapped Adam on the shoulder. "Listen, there's something I need to ask you, but maybe we should talk somewhere else?"

"It's okay," Adam said. "She's cool."

Beth wasn't sure whether that meant he trusted her to hear anything—or he didn't care what she thought.

"Yeah, okay. So . . ." Jake shifted his weight and scratched the side of his head, stalling. "The thing is, you probably know I took Harper Grace to the prom, right?"

Adam's jaw muscles tightened. Jake wouldn't have noticed, but Beth did. "Yeah, I heard."

"So when I went, I didn't realize the two of you were . . . you know."

"We're not," Adam said quickly.

"Right. I just wanted to check in with you, because . . ."

Beth didn't want Adam to realize she was staring, but she couldn't look away. He didn't look angry or upset. He looked . . . still. Like he'd put a tight lid on his emotions and he wasn't going to let a single one of them bubble to the surface.

"I thought I'd go for it," Jake finally said.

A muscle at the corner of Adam's eye twitched. "Why tell me?"

"I just wanted to make sure you were okay with it. You know, bros before hos and all that. Not that Harper's a—I didn't mean—"

"It's fine," Adam said. He grabbed Beth's hand, squeezing it so tight that it hurt. "Good to see you, Jake."

"You too!" Jake said, too heartily, but Adam had already

turned away, dragging Beth into the surging crowd.

"You okay?" she asked hesitantly, not sure if she wanted to hear the answer.

"Fine," he growled. "Let's go find the keg."

"Did Isabelle Peters always have such pretty eyes?" Kane asked, nodding at the quiet, first-chair violinist who was leaning against the mantel and falling out of her low-cut red corset top.

Miranda followed his gaze. "Those aren't her eyes," she said sourly.

"I'm going to go say hello," Kane said, staring shamelessly. Miranda stared too, wondering how the girl could breathe.

"Do you even *know* Isabelle Peters?" she asked, but Kane was already heading across the room. Miranda hurried to keep up, feeling like a fool. She'd been following him around all night, even though he'd barely spoken to her, much less looked at her. She told herself he was just in a bad mood.

Apparently, his mood had cleared just in time for him to flash a brilliant smile at Isabelle Peters, who blushed so deeply, her face clashed with her shirt.

"That was a beautiful violin solo you did at the spring concert this year," Kane said. Both girls gaped at him.

"I . . . I didn't know you were there," Isabelle stammered.

"Neither did *I*," Miranda said pointedly, since as far as she knew, Kane hadn't attended a school concert since giving up the trombone in the fourth grade.

"It was mesmerizing," Kane said. He took Isabelle's

right hand and laid it across his left palm, running his right hand lightly over her fingers. "To think that your ordinary hand could create such magic . . ."

"Um—um—" Isabelle ripped her hand away. "I should, uh, I have to go find my, uh, boyfriend. He's somewhere, I should, oh—" She was still muttering to herself as she hurried away.

Miranda couldn't help but laugh. "I guess your magic was too powerful for her," she teased.

Kane scowled. "What's that supposed to mean?"

"What? I was just—"

"What are you, jealous?" Kane sneered. And this wasn't the playful smirk she'd grown to know and love. This was full-blown disgust. "So now I'm not allowed to talk to other girls at all, is that it?"

"What are you talking about?" Miranda asked.

"You don't own me, you do realize that, right?"

"Why would I want to own you?" Miranda reached out for him, for his hand, his shoulder, but he pushed her away. "Kane, what's going on with you tonight?"

"Nothing." He rolled his eyes. "How about we stop analyzing everything I do for once, okay? I'm getting a drink." He turned away from her and headed abruptly toward the keg.

"Nothing for me, thanks," Miranda said sarcastically, knowing he couldn't hear.

She sat down on one of the couches, narrowly avoiding a puddle of spinach dip that was seeping into the brown leather. The party swirled on around her. Miranda waved to some friends, but couldn't muster up the will to actually talk to any of them. Not even Harper, whom she spotted by the dining room table, holding court over a gaggle of admirers but, at least to Miranda's trained eye, sulking and miserable. Harper was the last person she wanted to talk to right now, since she would have had to admit that her boyfriend was treating her like crap, and Harper would have wondered why she was putting up with it.

Maybe he's finally figured out I'm not good enough for him, Miranda thought.

But it wasn't her own voice she was hearing. It was her mother's. Inside her own head. And the self-pity and self-doubt backed off, replaced by outrage.

You don't deserve this, another voice pointed out. This one was Harper's, and it was angry. *Why are you letting him treat you this way?*

Miranda stood up and stalked into the kitchen, where a herd of frat-boys-in-training were working on their keg stands. Kane was, as usual, standing off to the sidelines, watching the action. And to an outside observer, it was obvious what was going on: The guys were performing for him, even if they wouldn't have admitted it to themselves. Trying to impress him, just like everyone else.

"Kane, can I talk to you for a sec?" she asked, tugging at his sleeve. *Don't ask—tell.* But there was difficult, and then there was impossible. Miranda was doing her best.

"Kinda busy here," he said, without taking his eyes off the pathetic keg action.

"Busy doing what?"

"Who wants to know?"

"How about your *girlfriend*?"

And now he did look at her, and she recoiled, because there was nothing in his eyes but scorn.

Steady, her inner Harper cautioned. *Hold your ground.*

Better fix this before he dumps you out with the trash, her mother's voice argued.

Miranda almost laughed. Was she going to lose her boyfriend and her mind all in the same night?

"Kane, this sucks," she finally said. "I'm ready to go home."

He looked at her again, like he'd forgotten she was even there. "Cool. Good luck finding a ride."

Miranda opened her mouth, but nothing came out.

It's your car—let him *find a ride.* But he was the one with the keys, and she was too embarrassed to force the issue.

Stay. If you walk out now, you might not get another shot. But she couldn't. She couldn't do that to herself, not even for Kane.

"Fine. I'm out of here," she spit out. "Have a good night."

Kane smiled at her for the first time that night—no, more like leered. "Oh, I will."

He wasn't drunk enough, not yet. But the beer tasted like ass, the punch rotted his teeth, and his stomach was staging a mutiny.

Having fun yet? Kane asked himself, and even his mental voice was sardonic. A party packed with hot girls, free booze, empty bedrooms, drunken seniors willing to do almost anything now that the end was in sight—it was supposed to be everything he'd ever wanted, but he could barely muster a smile.

And you know why.

Kane told himself to shut up. He'd never been the kind

to be bothered by inner voices; no point in starting now.

He pushed through the crowd and burst out onto the front lawn, which was mostly empty—all the action, more illicit by the minute, was out back, shielded from prying neighborly eyes. It's where Kane should have been. But he stayed in the front, walking the perimeter of the lawn, trying not to think.

And then he saw the perfect excuse to shut down his brain.

Harper. In a silver halter top and knee-high red leather boots with stiletto heels, leaning against a tree, looking hot and miserable. Looking like she didn't want to be alone.

"Hail, Harper, full of Grace," he greeted her, propping an arm against the tree trunk just over her head so that their bodies were only a few inches apart.

"Geary," she said wearily. "Just the man I didn't want to see. Where's Miranda?"

"I am not my girlfriend's keeper," he intoned solemnly.

"Just full of bullshit tonight, aren't you?"

"I aim to please," he said proudly. "Speaking of which, you're looking pretty pleasing yourself, Grace."

"Yeah, thanks."

"No." He touched her chin gently, then ran his hand through her wavy hair. "I mean, you look *good*. You're in a different league from the rest of these girls. You always have been."

"What the hell are you doing?"

He didn't know what he was doing. He was drunk, he told himself, so it didn't matter. It didn't count. He grabbed her hand. "Tell me you've never thought about it, Grace.

You, me—who else deserves us? Who else can understand our evil genius?"

She looked up at him, her lips moist and shimmery, slightly parted, giving him that look, and he was sure it meant desire. It meant *go*.

He lunged in for the kiss. And he must have been even drunker than he thought, because when she thrust out her arms and pushed him backward, he stumbled off balance and slammed into the ground, ass-first.

"What's wrong with you, slimeball?" she asked, standing over him. There was no anger on her face or in her voice. Just . . . Kane refused to acknowledge that it was pity. She wouldn't dare.

"I'm fine, thanks for asking," he said, examining his limbs and joints with exaggerated concern. "No major injuries."

She sat down next to him and gave him a light shove. "Obviously you must have hit your head at some point."

"Funny."

"I get what you're doing," Harper said.

He gave her what was supposed to be a withering stare, but Harper wasn't much for withering. "I wasn't aware I was doing anything."

"Miranda told me what she said to you on Saturday night. All that schmoopy stuff about how happy she was."

Kane grimaced. What was it with girls and their bottomless need to *talk*? Couldn't some things be left unsaid?

"She said she was afraid she screwed things up and scared you off, but then you were great about it and convinced her that everything was okay." Harper clapped him on the back.

"I didn't want to be the bearer of bad news, but . . ."

"But?"

"But I know you, Geary, and I know you've got to be freaking out."

Kane didn't respond.

"It's just like you to freak out in such a pathetic, piggish way." She laughed. "What were you thinking—that you'd come on to me, I'd tell Miranda and she'd break up with you, and it would save you from the horror of having an actual relationship?"

"Maybe I just thought you looked hot," Kane said.

Harper grinned. "You thought right. But I know you, Geary. Even you aren't *that* sleazy."

Kane sighed and leaned back on his elbows, tipping his head back so far, it nearly brushed against the grass. "So . . . are you going to tell her?"

"Do you want me to?"

She's just a girl, he reminded himself. *I should be able to take her or leave her.*

But he didn't want to leave her, and that's what scared him.

"No," he admitted.

"Then I won't. But keep in mind I'm not doing this for you," Harper said. "And if you screw up again—"

"I know."

"I think you're terrible for her," Harper told him. "But . . ."

"But?" he prompted.

"But who am I to know anything?" she asked, flopping forward and resting her head in her hands. "Look at me. I'm totally screwed up."

Kane knew she wouldn't have admitted it to anyone else—and probably wouldn't have admitted it to him, either, if he hadn't just entered into her debt. It was why he respected her. "You look pretty good, from where I'm sitting."

Harper laughed bitterly. "Yeah, well, from where I'm sitting, it looks like my life is crap. Everything that's happened this year . . ."

"Kaia," he said quietly. They never said her name, not anymore.

She nodded. "You'd think I'd be dying for this year to end, but . . ." She glared at him. "Swear you won't tell anyone, ever."

He held up a hand like he was swearing in at court. "Scout's honor."

"Like they'd let you into the Boy Scouts," she scoffed.

"Hey, I got six merit badges!" he said defensively. "And was working on a seventh . . . when they threw me out for hitting on the Scoutmaster's wife."

"Pig."

"Thank you."

"I'm terrified," she admitted. "Next year, leaving everything behind, everyone . . . it scares the shit out of me." She looked at him nervously, waiting for some response to the bombshell.

"No, it doesn't," he said.

"Geary, I'm baring my soul here. You don't get to tell me I'm wrong."

"You're not scared," he argued. "You're Harper Grace. Nothing scares you."

"Yeah, right." She looked over her shoulder. "Where are the cameras, Dr. Phil?"

"You need some self-actualization crap?" he teased. "Repeat after me: I am Harper Grace, and—"

"Shut up." She punched him lightly on the shoulder. "This is serious. I'm telling you how I feel."

"And I'm telling you to shove it." Kane was starting to feel like himself again. It was so much easier to have all the answers when you were dealing with someone else's life. "You're not scared. That's just your excuse not to go after what you want."

"And what is it I want?"

He gave her a disappointed look and clucked his tongue. "Grace, I thought we were being honest here."

"I don't—"

"Three days to graduation," he pointed out. "Clock's ticking. If you want Adam, he's right inside. Just go get him."

"Right inside with Beth," she reminded him.

Kane smacked the ground. "Get over it! So he can't get Queen of the Blands out of his system. Since when do you just accept that and walk away?"

"Since he chose a murderer over me," Harper murmured. "He had his chance. I can't go chasing after him. And even if I did, soon he won't even . . ."

"What?"

"Nothing."

Kane sighed. "Look, I don't know what your problem is, and it's not like I'm qualified to hand out relationship advice. Maybe you're right, and you can't have him. It doesn't mean you should just lie down and play dead."

"So what do you suggest?"

"Since when do you need my suggestions?" He

grabbed her by the shoulders and gave her a sharp shake. "Forget about Adam—go find someone else. Or a bunch of someone elses. Have some fun again. You may not have noticed, but we're at a party."

"Yeah, you seem to be having a hell of a good time."

"We're talking about you," he said. "And you love parties. Last I checked, you love men. And, most of all, you love the idea of getting the hell out of Grace, CA, and starting your real life. It's all you've been talking about since first grade. So don't tell me you're scared. Just figure out what you really want, and go get it. You're Harper Grace. That's what you do."

Harper gaped at him.

"What?" he said finally. "Did I sprout a third eye?"

She balled up her fist and he flinched, half expecting her to punch him again, but instead she just rapped sharply on his chest. "Why, Tin Man," she said, dripping with sweetness, "I do believe you may finally have grown a heart."

"Great," he said sourly. "Does that make you the brainless scarecrow or the gutless lion?"

She wiggled her legs in the air and clicked the heels of her red leather boots together. "Get a clue. I'm Dorothy."

Kane stood up and brushed off the grass. "Then click your heels together for me a few more times, would you? Because I'm heading home."

"Kane—" She jumped up and grabbed his arm.

"Yeah?"

"What you said . . . thanks. But as long as we're dishing out the advice—"

"Who said *we* were dishing out anything?"

"As long as we're dishing out the advice," she said again, louder, "here's some for you. I may need to go after what I want, but you . . . all that crap you think you want?" She jerked her head toward the party, toward the girls and the booze and the drugs and the fun. "Do you really want it more than what you've already got?"

Kane shook off her arm. "I'm going home, Oprah. So unless you want to come along . . ."

"Don't throw away something good just because you think you can do better," Harper said quietly. "And I'm not just saying that for her. I'm saying it for you."

"So what do you think? Ad? Did you hear me?"

He shook his head. He hadn't heard. He still wasn't hearing. He was just seeing. Her.

Adam wasn't trying to watch her. He was trying *not* to watch her. But she was everywhere, and he couldn't stop himself. It was like he had an internal radar that *pinged* every time Harper glided across his field of vision.

Ping. There she was, moping in a corner.

Ping. There she was, fending off Jake Oberman.

Ping. There she was, disappearing out the door—and he'd hoped she had left for the night, that he was finally going to get some relief.

But then she returned, a wide smile on her face. She strode across the room, with purpose, toward him—he thought, at first—but then past him, to Jake. Adam watched. He couldn't help it. Harper didn't even notice. She was on a mission. Jake looked up, smiled. Harper grabbed a fistful of his shirt, tugged him toward her. They kissed.

Ping.

"Adam, what are you . . . oh." Beth's voice trailed off.

Harper had obviously caught Jake by surprise, but it hadn't taken him long to rally. They were locked together, Harper up on her toes and Jake's long fingers roaming across her back, veering down, cupping her—

"Bastard!" Adam hissed, and took a step. Then stopped himself. Beth put a hand on his arm, and he forced himself not to shake it off. His blood burned. How dare he—how dare *she*? And right in front of him . . . Adam knew he wasn't allowed to be angry.

He didn't care.

He wanted to storm over there, grab Harper out of Jake's hands, punch Jake in the gut, sling Harper over his shoulder, and run away.

Maybe punch Jake in the gut *and* face, he thought, watching the guy practically undress Harper while everyone watched. But then definitely grab her and head for the hills.

Maybe she's drunk, he told himself. *Maybe he's taking advantage, and she needs rescuing.* But Adam, better than anyone, knew that Harper wasn't drunk. After all, he'd been watching her all night. He'd counted the beers, followed her steps, monitored every move out of the corner of his eye. She wasn't drunk. Not yet, at least.

And when had Harper Grace ever needed rescuing?

No, he didn't want to save her. He just *wanted* her—and he hadn't realized how much, until right now.

"Ad? Are you okay?" Beth asked.

It was only then that he remembered she was there. She was there with *him*. He couldn't run across the room and . . . do anything, not with Beth by his side. Was he supposed to abandon her to pull some caveman stunt that would probably just make Harper laugh?

"Do you want to take off?" she asked.

He ripped himself away from Harper and Jake and turned to face his date—not allowing himself to wonder whether he was here with the wrong girl. He was here with the one he had to be with. And it's not like Harper had given him much of a choice. "Don't you have to stay?" he asked, though he did want to leave, and now, before he did something stupid. Or would it be stupider to do nothing? He glanced at Harper again, who had finally detached herself, at least for the moment. She looked strange, and it took him a moment to figure out why. She looked happy. "Shouldn't you stick around? You know, the picture thing?"

Beth gave him a weird look. "I gave my camera to that guy Mike, from the basketball team, don't you remember? It was your idea, you said I'd get better pictures that way if I handed it off?"

Adam shrugged. He'd been too busy watching Harper to pay attention to much else. "Right. Sure."

"I should probably stick around and keep an eye on it, but . . ." She rested her hand against his lower back, offering him support. "It doesn't matter. If you want to go."

"You can stay," he offered. "I'll grab a ride—"

"You shouldn't go alone," she said. "I'll come."

She was trying to support *him*. Adam almost laughed. While he'd been standing there thinking about ditching her to go make some kind of scene with Harper. Harper, who had barely looked in his direction all night long.

I'm an idiot, he thought angrily. *A selfish idiot.*

Harper was the one who'd forced a choice, and Adam had made it. Now they both had to live with the consequences. Adam had promised himself that he would stand by Beth no matter what. And if "no matter what" included Harper sucking face with some asshole from Crestview, well . . . there was nothing he could do about it. Not without breaking his promise.

Adam had broken enough of those for one year.

"So should we get out of here?" Beth asked.

He slipped his hand around hers, and she gave it a gentle squeeze. "Let's go home."

The noise burrowed into her, spurted out of her, swung her around, and sent her sailing. Not just the music, a rocking beat that made Harper want to fling her arms wide and spin, bashing her head back and forth, her hair flying. It was everything. The shouts, the cries, the laughter, the hoots, the hollers, the giggles, the whispers and murmurs and drunken shrieks all mixing together into a single voice and it was *her* voice, and Harper sensed that if she opened her mouth, it would all flow out of her, the excitement, the wild, the *party*.

The life of the party. The phrase finally made sense to her. The party itself was alive, a churning mass of twisting bodies and toothy grins, and Harper was at the center of it all, letting it raise her up. What had she been doing, slinking around in corners, wasting her chance to touch and taste everything the party had to offer?

There was the boy, Jake, and it felt so good to be wanted again, to know exactly what to do to make him need her—and then to leave him behind, begging for more. She couldn't give it to him; she couldn't waste any more time on one person. She owed it to the party to be free, to be wild, uncontained and unrestrained. She let the motion of the crowd carry her, let the glasses pass through her hand, slugged back their contents, swallowing the warm, bitter liquid until it made her brain buzz.

She didn't drink to forget or to lose herself or to hide—she drank because it was there, and *she* was there, fully, finally, and she wasn't wasting it, not anymore. She could do anything, and she could do it on her own, without him, without anybody, because she was Harper Grace and that was all she needed to be happy.

And when hands grabbed hers and pulled her up onto a table, she followed their lead and shined under the stares and the cheers, and the flashes in the crowd made her feel like a star, like she had an entourage and a fleet of paparazzi just trying to catch up, and now they had, and she was going to give them a show. The music surged and she sang along, because she could, and pulled off her shirt and swung it in the air because it was hot and so was she and because she wanted to—and that's what the night was about. And then Jake was up on the table next to her, he'd found her again and his kiss was even better the second time around.

"I need you," he whispered, and she couldn't hear the words but she could read his lips, and it felt good to be needed, but she didn't need him—didn't need anyone—so she kissed him again and then pushed him away, off the table, because it was hers alone. It was her party, it was her night—she was Harper Grace, it was her world, and she was finally ready to stake her claim.

chapter

9

Kane stood on the doorstep, holding his fist a few inches from the door. There was still time to change his mind and make a quick getaway. He could end this thing right here and now before he got in any deeper.

He knocked.

Miranda's mother opened the door, and Kane did his best to smile. Mrs. Stevens, on the other hand, was beaming. "It's *so* wonderful to see you again," she gushed. "I hope Miranda's taking good care of you—you've been so good to her."

Kane nodded. "Is she home?"

"Miranda!" She bellowed a couple more times and, finally, there was an irritated response.

"What?"

"Come down here. It's your boyfriend!"

Silence. Mrs. Stevens gave Kane an awkward smile and patted him on the shoulder. "She's probably just getting a late start this morning. I'll go up and see what the trouble is."

"I can come back another time . . ."

"No! Oh, no!" She pulled him inside and slammed the door behind him, as if afraid he'd escape, then bustled upstairs. A few moments later, Miranda appeared.

She didn't say anything to Kane, didn't even look at him as she walked past, opened the door, and stepped outside. He didn't move, not until she turned around and glared. "Are you coming?"

Kane followed her out.

"I can't talk when *she's* breathing down my neck," Miranda muttered. She leaned against the porch railing. "What do you want?"

Kane paused. Smooth-talking was, of course, his specialty—but suddenly he didn't know what to say. "I thought you might want your car back."

Miranda pursed her lips. "I said you could have it for the week, and you can have it for the week. I don't say things I don't mean."

The implication was clear: *Unlike* some *people*.

"Can we go somewhere?" he asked, squeezing his fist around the keys. The metal bit sharply into the flesh of his palm.

"Where?"

"Just . . . you know. For a drive." He needed to talk—but if he was behind the wheel, he could say what he needed to say without looking at her. And she wouldn't be able to leave.

"Fine."

They walked to the car and though he hurried to open her door, she anticipated him and got there first, shutting it without a word. He got into the driver's seat, and they pulled away.

"I'm sorry about last night, Stevens," he finally said, once they'd gotten onto the open highway. "I was an asshole."

"The biggest," she agreed. "What gives?"

Kane tried one of his patented adorable grins. "Can I plead temporary insanity?"

Miranda turned her face away, staring out the window at the empty desert streaming by. "If you don't want to be with me, just say it," she said, with only a hint of a waver. "You don't need to put on this elaborate show. If you want to break up, let's break up. It's fine."

"It's not fine." He didn't take his eyes off the road, but he reached across the seat and took her hand. "Stevens, it's *not* fine. I don't want to break up."

"Then *what?*" she asked, putting his hand firmly back on the gear shift. "You can't just treat me like crap and then show up the next day and pretend nothing happened."

Focus on the road, he told himself. *Just pretend she's not even in the car.*

"I got freaked," he admitted. "All that stuff you said, I just . . . I got freaked."

"Oh." They were both quiet for a moment. "Because you thought . . . Kane, I wasn't trying to, I mean, it's not like I said—" She took a deep breath. "I'm not trying to pressure you. I really didn't mean anything."

"Don't say that." He pressed down harder on the gas pedal, wishing he could outrun the conversation. Or just fast-forward a few minutes so that he wouldn't actually have to live through it. "I'm glad you said it. You know, that this is making you happy. That we're—I'm glad. This is good, Stevens. What we've got here?" He took her hand again, and this time she let him. "It's good. And I don't want to screw it up."

"You didn't," she said softly.

"I wish I could . . ." Kane sighed. "I'm just not that kind of guy. We're not going to sit here and talk about my feelings and shit. I don't do that."

Miranda laughed, and the sound made something in him unclench. He relaxed his hold on the wheel. "Don't you think I know that? Kane, I've watched you spout Shakespearean sonnets to impress some illiterate who thought you wrote them yourself. Do you really think I'd believe you if you started telling me that my lips were like rubies and comparing me to a summer's day? Do you really think I *want* that?"

"So what *do* you want?"

"Nothing," she said. "I'm not asking anything of you— I mean, it would be good if you never treated me like crap again, but that doesn't seem like too much to ask, right?"

"I think I can handle it," Kane said. He knew he should push her harder—she had to want something more from him. Or if she didn't, she should. She deserved to demand something from him, from their relationship. But if she was going to pretend otherwise, he wasn't going to press the issue. "So am I forgiven?"

Miranda raised his hand to her lips and began kissing his fingertips. "Somehow I suspect you'll find a way to make it up to me. . . ."

He was about to suggest one when the cop car appeared in his rearview mirror, its siren blaring.

Kane glanced down at the speedometer. "Damn." He veered toward the side of the road and pulled to a stop, mildly irritated at the prospect of a ticket—until he remembered what he had in the trunk. Then, suddenly, a ticket seemed like a small price to pay.

He wiped his palms on his jeans and then rolled down the window. *Just give me the ticket and walk away,* he silently implored the cop. *Nice and easy.* Miranda had already pulled the registration out of the glove compartment and handed it to Kane, giving him a sympathetic smile, like they had nothing to worry about but a minor inconvenience.

"You know how fast you were going, son?" the cop asked, his sunglasses so large, they nearly covered up his pencil-thin mustache. Kane didn't recognize him, which meant he wasn't one of the usual traffic cops. He took a closer look at the uniform, feeling bile rise in his throat—state police?

"I'm very sorry, Officer," Kane simpered, handing over his license and registration. "It won't happen again."

"This your car, son?"

Kane resisted the urge to tell him to shove the "son" talk. *Play nice,* he warned himself. "It's my girlfriend's car, sir." He nodded at Miranda.

The cop tipped his hat to her. "Then maybe your *girlfriend* can tell me why there's an empty bottle of beer in the backseat."

Oh, shit. "I don't know how that got there," Kane said quickly, which was true. He'd given some guys a ride home the night before, and one of the idiots must have used the car as his own personal dump truck. "Really."

"Sure you don't." The officer's lip curled up in a sneer eerily similar to the one Kane usually wore. "But all the same, I'm going to have to ask you two to get out of the car so I can take a closer look."

"I don't think you have the right to—"

"Kane!" Miranda hissed. "Just let him do his job so we can get out of here."

He nodded and gave her a tight smile. They climbed out of the car and were escorted to the cop car, where they were told to stand still and watch as the cop searched Miranda's Civic for more contraband. Kane berated himself with every curse word he'd ever learned. How could he have been so stupid?

"Chill out," Miranda whispered. "It's going to be okay. I don't think they can do anything to us for an empty bottle."

And then the cop opened the trunk.

Game over.

"Well, well, well," the cop drawled. "What's this you've got in here?"

"What?" Miranda asked. "I don't have anything in there—" She started toward the car, but the cop held up his arms.

"I'm sorry, but I'm going to have to ask you to stand by the car, miss," he said, looking not the slightest bit sorry. "In fact, judging from what I see here, I think I'm going to have to run you both down to the station."

"What's he talking about?" Miranda asked Kane, looking panicked. "What's in the trunk?"

Kane didn't say anything. Miranda leaned against him and put an arm around his waist. He couldn't move, not even to comfort her. Not even to step away.

The cop approached.

"Sir, I don't know anything about something in the trunk," Miranda said nervously, her face flushed.

"Well, maybe that's true, and maybe it isn't, but someone's got to be held responsible. How about you, son?" His eyes bored into Kane. "You know anything about what's in that trunk? You want to take responsibility?"

This was his chance.

Actually, his *chance* had been that morning, when he could have taken the large cardboard box of pot candy out of the trunk *before* driving over to Miranda's. His chance had passed him on by. This was just his moment to minimize the damage. As the cop said, to take responsibility. Kane's gaze drifted down to the guy's holster, which contained a real gun. Kane talked big, but he'd never been this close to a gun before, so close that he could have reached out and made a grab for it.

The cop was drawing out a pair of handcuffs. At least those, Kane was familiar with. But before, he had always been the one holding the key. The cop swung the handcuffs back and forth, and Kane imagined how they might feel on his wrists. Miranda's arms tightened around him, and he could feel her shaking.

This was his moment.

"I'm sorry, Officer, but I have no idea what's in that trunk," he said, meeting the guy's eyes with a suitably apologetic smile. "This isn't even my car."

With only a couple days to go before graduation, school had become pretty much optional, which meant that Beth was free to drop the camera off at the *Grace Weekly Journal* offices midday. She was eager to see the journalists in action, struggling to meet their deadlines—but unfortunately, the office didn't seem that much busier than it had over the weekend.

Everyone she passed had a bored, sleepy look on their face as if they'd just interrupted a nap to do a few minutes of work before falling back asleep again. It didn't matter, she told herself. So what if it wasn't the *New York Times*? It was a start.

Ashley Statten, at least, looked wide awake. She leaped out of her chair when Beth approached, grabbing the camera out of her hands. "Finally! The article's all set and ready to lock, I just need the photos." She hooked the camera up to her computer and began flipping through the images as Beth hovered nervously over her shoulder.

"Can you not do that?" Ashley asked, glaring.

"What?"

"I can't really concentrate with you standing there and—oh, forget it." She grabbed a few sheets of paper from her printer and shoved them into Beth's hands. "Why don't you sit over there, read this, and be quiet."

"What is it?" Beth asked.

Ashley rolled her eyes. "I can't imagine why you aren't already a prize-winning journalist, what with those stellar investigative skills." She tapped the top of the page. "As this rather large clue in the shape of a headline will tell you, it's an advance copy of the article. Enjoy."

Beth settled into the designated chair and began to read.

BEAUTY AS THE BEAST: THE RISE AND FALL OF A HIGH SCHOOL DRAMA QUEEN

By Ashley Statten

Photos by Beth Manning

Harper Grace and Kaia Sellers had it all. Beauty. Popularity. Power. High school remains the country's last monarchy, and at Haven High, Harper Grace and Kaia Sellers reigned as queens. But no golden age lasts forever. Camelot ended with a tragic car crash that left one girl dead and raised endless questions about the disturbing underbelly of Grace's youth culture. Allegations of student-teacher liaisons, blackmail, and drug use abound—and at the center of it all stand two girls, picture perfect, their glossy hair and pretty smiles hiding the dark truth.

Beth gasped and, her heartbeat quickening, skimmed through the article, which got worse with every sentence.

"She's a royal bitch," one senior, who preferred to remain anonymous for fear of retribution, claimed about Harper Grace. "She's got no soul. Ask anyone. She thinks we all worship her—but that'd be like worshipping the devil."

How did she get all this? Beth wondered, incredulous as she read Ashley's rundown of Harper's and Kaia's misdeeds, including a step-by-step explication of how Harper had, over the years, clawed her way to the top.

Ilana Hochstein, a psychologist specializing in the behavior of modern teens and author of the recent book *Out of Control*, asserts that "High school girls can be ruthless—they're masters of manipulation, backstabbing, anything you can think of to get ahead, they've done. There's rarely physical violence, but the emotional damage done can be far worse." Experts agree: Adolescent girls are weapons of mass destruction. And the cauldron of Haven High—a perfect storm of sex, drinking, and misbehavior—offered the perfect setting for Harper Grace and Kaia Sellers to practice their craft.

Beth tore through the rest of the article, terrified she was going to see her own name, but it was nowhere to be found. Just more sociological spewing about alpha females and the corruption of modern youth, all spiced up by tales from Haven High's very own "dark side," as personified by Harper and the dearly departed Kaia.

"Perfect!" Ashley exclaimed suddenly, enlarging a couple of the photos on her screen. "Maybe you've got a future in photography."

Beth didn't recognize the images—they must have been taken after she'd left, because certainly, she would have remembered this.

In the picture on the left, Harper stood on a table, topless, waving her shirt in midair, her mouth open as if in a silent scream. The picture on the right was similar, except that she had her tongue jammed down some guy's throat.

"I should caption this 'Portrait of the artist as a young slut,'" Ashley said, laughing, "but I guess that wouldn't fly with this crowd. What do you think, Beth? This is your world, after all."

"I don't—I think—" Beth stopped. If she got the internship, Ashley might be her boss. *If* she got the internship. If she didn't screw up and start pissing people off. If she just kept her mouth shut and let this go.

But even Beth wasn't that weak.

"I think this is libel," Beth said, slapping the pages down on the desk. "It's a total hatchet job. You can't just say this stuff about people—I mean, Kaia's *dead*, and Harper's just—she's a *person*. You can't just write this about her like she's not going to read it. This will kill her."

Beth expected the reporter to defend herself. But she just leaned back in her chair and smiled. "What do you care?"

"What do you mean? I care because—it's wrong. You can't write something like this and call it journalism. It's character assassination."

"What do I mean? I mean, what do you care what happens to Harper Grace? Didn't she ruin your life? Isn't she your worst enemy?"

Beth's eyes widened.

"Oh, I know everything," Ashley said snidely. "It's called journalism. You should try it sometime. I asked around, I know what she did to you. And what you did to her—"

Beth gasped—how could Ashley have found out about the drugs she'd slipped Harper? And if she knew, and she knew about the car accident . . .

"That stupid gossip flyer," Ashley said, making a *tsk*-ing noise. "I don't know why you thought that was going to work. But then, I guess that's why girls like Harper and Kaia walk all over you, isn't it? I'm thinking about making this part of a continuing series—maybe part two should be an exposé of the high school underclass. What do you think? You could give me an exclusive."

"You can't print this," Beth insisted. "I won't let you."

Ashley stuffed the pages and her notebooks into a drawer and shut down the file on her computer. "I don't see how you're going to stop me," she said calmly. "It's a done deal. In fact, with photos like these, I think it's pretty much guaranteed a page-one spot for our graduation edition. And just think—it's all thanks to you."

"I don't know anything about it!" Miranda said again, tears streaming down her face. "Why won't you believe me?"

"Because it's your car, miss," the detective said. "Which means that unless you can prove someone else put the contraband in there without your knowledge, it's your responsibility."

Miranda moaned. None of this seemed real. Not the tiny dark room with the long mirror along one wall, or the rosy-cheeked bald man sitting across from her informing her of her rights. Not the reddish rings around her wrists from where the handcuffs had chewed into her skin, or the sore muscles in her back from sitting in that chair, in that room, for hours, answering every question the same way.

I don't know.

But didn't she know? Didn't she know who *must* have put the box of pot-laced candy in her trunk—a big enough box, the man had helpfully informed her, to indicate intent-to-distribute, which apparently activated some kind of mandatory sentencing guidelines. In case she was found guilty, of course.

Sentencing guidelines.

Intent-to-distribute.

Guilty.

She was trapped in some horrible made-for-TV movie about good girls gone bad, and surely any moment now someone would arrive to change the channel. Surely, to be more specific, if the box belonged to Kane, then he would claim it. He wouldn't let her take the fall.

Take the fall. There was another line she'd heard only in prison movies. If this did turn out to be real and not some overly vivid nightmare from which she'd soon wake, she was going to need a whole new vocabulary.

"I'm sorry to inform you of this, miss," the man said

politely, grabbing her arm and pulling her out of the chair. Her legs barely supported her. "But you have the right to remain silent. Anything you say can and will—"

"Wait," Miranda said desperately. "I didn't do anything. Please."

But the man had continued through her interruption, and was already at the part about court-provided attorneys.

What about my right to a phone call? Miranda wondered through her horror. *When does he get to that?*

But he never did. First there was the fingerprinting. She'd done it once before, in third grade, as some kind of state-supported missing-children program. *Get your kid in the system,* the teachers had advised, *and you'll always be able to find her.*

They'll always be able to track me down, Miranda now thought. If, for example, she went to prison, then escaped. She'd be in the "system" forever.

She told herself to stop running movies in her head and start figuring her way out of her mess, but there was no way out. The man's grip on her arm was firm. He grabbed each finger in turn, pressed it into the inkpad, then smashed it onto the little white piece of paper. Then they dragged her away, her hands still stained with black.

It was picture time.

Just like when she'd gotten her driver's license, she stood on the blue tape square, in front of the white screen, and stared at the tiny box camera. *Am I supposed to smile?* she thought stupidly, but then the camera flashed, and it was over.

"We've got to fix up a cell for you," the cop told her, not harshly, but not gently, either. "You can call whoever you need to, then Carrie here will take you into the waiting area until we're ready."

Miranda started trembling. *This isn't real, this isn't real, this isn't real,* she repeated to herself, her lips moving, though no sound came out. She forced herself to stop thinking about where she was and what came next, because if she did, her mind would tear apart, she could feel it already, straining, fault lines crackling across the surface. She just needed to obey orders and put one foot in front of the other. Survive.

The pay phone was sticky. Miranda held it between two fingers and tried not to touch it to her ear or mouth. They gave her a couple quarters.

Harper didn't answer the phone. And Miranda couldn't bear to leave a message. Not this message.

The next one was worse.

"Mom?"

"Miranda, where are you? I was expecting you back hours ago, I need to run out and your sister can't stay here by yourself, and you're just off with your boyfriend somewhere? I thought we'd talked about responsibility—"

"Mom!" Deep breaths, Miranda told herself. Just say it. "Something . . . happened."

"Was there an accident?" her mother asked, and Miranda was surprised to hear the concern in her voice. It sounded almost . . . maternal. And it gave her a little courage.

"I'm actually, uh, down at the police station," she said quietly, humiliated.

"What happened?" The concern was gone.

"We got stopped. For speeding. And, uh, the cops

found some, uh, drugs in the trunk—but they're not mine!" she said quickly, before her mother could ask.

"Oh, Miranda, what have you gotten yourself into?"

"Mom, I told you, it wasn't—"

"Something like this could ruin your future," her mother complained. "How many times have I told you to *think* before you act?"

"That's what I'm trying to tell you, Mom, I *didn't* act. I didn't do anything."

"Then why did they arrest you?"

"I don't know!" Miranda shouted. "But why don't you take my side for once in my life and *believe* me!"

"Don't you take that tone with me!" her mother snapped. "Now you see where that kind of disrespect for authority will get you."

"You think I'm in *jail* because I talk back to my mother too much?" Miranda asked incredulously. The familiar rhythm of their mother-daughter sniping was actually helping to calm her down. It was comforting to know that even *here*, her relationship with her mother was a constant. Constant dysfunction—but beggars couldn't be choosers.

"What I think is that this whole thing is extremely disturbing."

"You think *you're* disturbed?" Miranda forced herself to stop. She lowered her voice. "Look, Mom, I need a lawyer—I need to get out of here."

"Do you know how much that would cost?" her mother asked. "Won't they give you one for free?"

"I guess, but—" The cop had explained that would probably take at least another day; Grace wasn't Los

Angeles, with public defenders lining the court hallways, waiting for the next defendant to pop off the assembly line. There were only two or three lawyers who served regularly across the county, which sometimes meant long delays. Especially when the case was so minor. It didn't feel minor to Miranda. "Mom, I need to get out *now*. I can't stay here—I can't sleep in a cell!"

"It won't be so bad," her mother said. "You have to learn that your actions have consequences. I'll talk to your father—I don't know how I'm going to break this to him—and we'll talk to you in the morning."

"Mom, *please*." She was disgusted with herself for whimpering, but there was nothing she could do about it.

"Oh, don't be so dramatic. It's one night, it's not going to kill you. We'll work it all out in the morning."

"Mom—!"

Dial tone.

Carrie, receptionist-cum-prison guard, escorted her to the "waiting room," which was really just a narrow room with peeling yellow walls about the size of her bedroom. It was filled with rows and rows of chairs, like a bus terminal waiting area, but they were all empty. All except for one, in the corner.

She sat down in a seat against the left wall. Carrie sat across from her. "I'm supposed to cuff you," she said. "But I think it's okay. Not like you're going to run, right?" She laughed.

"Right," Miranda agreed, managing a weak smile.

Carrie nodded toward the back corner. "You can talk to him, if you want." When she smiled, the thickly applied bright red lipstick made her look a bit like an evil clown.

Miranda didn't want. But apparently Kane did. He slid into the chair next to her, then flashed Carrie a winning smile. "Is it okay if we talk privately for a minute?"

Carrie blushed. "Sure, I guess that'd be fine." She moved a few seats away, never taking her eyes off Miranda.

Kane put his hands on her shoulders and began to massage. She wanted to knock them away, but she couldn't move.

"I'm so sorry," he whispered. "Are you okay?"

"It was you, wasn't it?" she asked coldly. "They're yours."

"Stevens, I never expected this to happen—"

"Tell them the truth," she pleaded. "Just get me out of here."

He leaned closer, his lips against her ear. She shuddered at the touch. "This isn't such a big deal, Stevens. It's your first offense, you'll get off with a slap on the wrist, trust me."

"Funny, it feels like a big deal to me."

"They're just doing this to scare you, I promise. They're bored, and this gives them a chance to play big-city cop for the day. But nothing's going to happen to you; I won't let it."

"And how are you going to stop it when you're at home in bed tonight and I'm here, *behind bars*?" She glanced down at his fingers—no ink. She was alone in this. And he could give her all the massages and whispered assurances he wanted, but he wasn't going to change that. He *could*, but he wouldn't. She understood that now.

Or rather, she knew it. She would never understand it.

Something incomprehensible blared on Carrie's walkie-talkie. She held it to her ear, then nodded. "I gotta take you back now," she said apologetically, gesturing for Miranda to stand up. Kane stood too. He tried to give Miranda a kiss, but she turned her face away.

Carrie gripped her upper arm and guided her toward the door. "You can check back tomorrow about bail," she told him.

"Miranda, it's going to be okay," Kane said. "I promise."

His face looked different than she'd ever seen it. Without the smirk and the arched eyebrows, it looked naked. Defenseless.

"I'm going to fix this," he said.

The dam burst, and tears streamed down her face. She didn't want to look at him, but she didn't want to look away because when he left, she would be alone. And soon there would be bars.

"Miranda, *look at me*," he insisted. "Believe me. It's going to be okay."

"Kane—" She gasped for breath. "Please!"

Please do the right thing.

Please sacrifice yourself to save me.

But if that's what she wanted, she'd chosen the wrong boyfriend. She knew that as well as he did. At least, she did now. Miranda had always claimed she knew Kane, knew what she was getting into. But secretly, she'd always thought she knew better. That beneath the blasé bluster, there was something real. Something good.

"I'm sorry," he said, his voice husky. "*Miranda*, I'm sorry." And then, as Carrie pulled her through the door, he turned away first, like he couldn't watch them take her away. "I just can't."

"Don't give me that bullshit!" Harper screamed, and there was a thud that sounded like she was throwing her entire body at the door. "Let me *in*!"

Kane grabbed his shoe and threw it at the front door, wishing it was Harper's head. "I told you, I'm busy. Go away."

"Busy? Your girlfriend's in *jail*, asshole! Now *let! Me! In!*"

Kane sighed and opened the door. Maybe this was his punishment. If so, it wasn't nearly what he deserved. But it was a start.

"Why are you here, Grace?" he asked wearily, settling down into one of the living room couches. Not the couch he'd been lying on for the past three hours, staring up at the ceiling and wondering what the hell was wrong with him. It was time for a change of scenery.

"Good question, Geary," she spit out, pacing back and forth. "Why *am* I here? Why aren't I at home sleeping off my hangover? Why did I get dragged out of bed to go visit my *best friend* in *prison*?"

"You saw her?" he asked, leaning forward. "How is she?"

"No, asshole, I didn't see her, they wouldn't let me until tomorrow. They're big on the rules there, you know, in *prison*."

"Stop saying that. It's not prison. It's just the police station."

"It might as well be prison. Is she locked in a cell? Are there bars? Is she stuck in some shithole sharing a bunkbed with a hooker?"

"How am I supposed to know?"

"Exactly." Harper stopped pacing and glared down at him. "You wouldn't know. Because you're not there. *She* is. And you just let it happen."

"What makes you think this is my fault?"

"*Drugs* in her car? Intent to distribute?" Harper kicked at the couch, narrowly missing his legs. "They're *yours*, Geary. What kind of a loser lets his girlfriend take the fall for him?"

As if he hadn't been asking himself the same question for hours.

He shrugged, and composed his face into the perfect image of apathy. "Look, Grace, whatever Miranda has or hasn't done, there's nothing I can do about it. It's not my problem."

"Not your *problem*?" Harper sat down across from him and leaned forward, no longer shouting. "Not your problem, Kane?" She shook her head. "I knew you were slime, but I always thought . . . what are you doing? How are you letting this happen?"

"Don't," he warned her, with an edge to his voice. "Don't try to pretend that you wouldn't do the same thing."

"Of course I—"

"Oh, please." He sneered at her, letting his anger rise because it was the only thing that would wash away all those other, messier emotions. "You and I are the same, Grace. We look out for ourselves. We take what we want, we don't care who gets hurt. You treat Miranda like shit whenever it serves your purposes, so don't come in here acting all noble."

"It's not the same."

"It *is* the same. We're the same. The only difference is, I *own* it. You like to pretend that you're better than all that, but when it comes down to a choice between your happiness and someone else's, don't tell me you don't choose your own. Every damn time. You want to call me slime? Take a look in the mirror sometime, Gracie, because it's oozing out of every pore."

Harper's face had gone white. She stood up. "You disgust me."

"That doesn't make me wrong."

She slammed the door behind her, and he was alone again. Kane opened his fist. He had been clutching his cell phone ever since he'd left the police station. With one call, he could end this. End it for Miranda, at least.

But for him, it would be the beginning of hell. There was no case against her. Charges would never stick. The car had been out of her possession for days. A fine, maybe. Community service, even. But nothing big. Nothing major.

Kane, on the other hand, already had a juvenile record. A trivial one, just minor infractions, but a record nonetheless. And Kane had connections—which, under the wrong circumstances, could become witnesses. Kane had everything to lose.

Miranda would be fine, he told himself. He'd find a way to fix things, without destroying himself in the process. He couldn't do that, even for her. He couldn't do it for anyone.

It doesn't make me evil, he told himself. *It just makes me human.*

Self-preservation was a fundamental human right. More than that—it was an obligation.

He wished he could be that guy, the one who could dial the number, confess to his crimes, and save the day. For the first time in his life, he wished he was someone else, someone nobler, someone braver. Someone better. But he wasn't.

This is who I am, he thought, finally putting down the phone. *Whatever it costs me.*

But this time, he wasn't the one who would pay.

chapter

10

Where do you see yourself in ten years?

It was a standard yearbook question, and everyone knew you were expected to supply a standard yearbook answer. The public answer—the short, snappy, wholesome answer that would appear next to your photo and send the message to your parents, teachers, friends, and enemies that you were normal. It was the generic answer, the nothing-to-see-here-folks quip that the eye skimmed over, it was "I'll be married with 2.5 kids," it was "I'll be a millionaire," it was "I'll work for my daddy's accounting firm," or "I'll win the lottery and buy the high school and turn it into a bowling alley," or "I'll be hanging out at the Playboy Mansion with my good friend Hef."

And it was a lie.

Because if you had enough brains to actually graduate from high school, it meant you'd never be stupid enough to tell the truth, to expose the dirty little secret of who you really were—and what you really wanted.

Harper lies under the silken canopy, her legs bare, her skin glowing, her neck draped with jewels.

"You may approach," she says languidly, when she hears the knock.

Adam rushes to her side, dropping to his knees and clasping her hand. He presses it to his lips. "I thought I would die without you," he says.

"You were only gone a day."

"One day too many." He caresses her cheek. "Every hour was agony. Every minute was a stake through my chest."

"So you missed me?" she asks, favoring him with a smile.

"It was as if a chunk of flesh had been torn away, as if someone carved out my heart and threw it on the ground," he says. He grabs her hands, and she rises to her feet. The kiss is magical.

"I love you," he tells her, his arms still around her. "I love you more than I ever thought possible. I'll love you forever."

"And if I ever asked you to do something for me, to give something up—"

"No sacrifice is too great," he says. "I would do anything for you. I would rather die than see you hurt."

"So I have your complete devotion?"

He kisses her again. "You have everything of me there is to give."

Harper rubbed the tears away from her eyes and tried to focus on the road. Kane was wrong: They weren't the same. They couldn't be. She was selfish, she knew that. But there was nothing wrong with wanting things. And there was nothing wrong with demanding what you knew you deserved.

She didn't want Adam to be her servant, didn't want

him to throw away his life for her. She just wanted to come first—she wanted him to love her more than he loved Beth, more than he loved basketball, more than anything. Yes, she wanted all of him . . . but only because she loved him so much.

Only because she was ready to give him all of her.

So Kane was wrong. It wasn't the same at all. Whatever she did, she did for love—love of someone else. Kane only loved himself.

Kane settles into the Jacuzzi, raises a glass of Cristal, and thinks how much he loves his life. It isn't just the thirty-room McMansion or the seventy acres of surrounding grounds, complete with tennis court, stables, swimming pool, and artificial waterfall. It isn't the seven-car garage with its rotating line-up of Porsches, Ferraris, Bentleys, and the one constant: a mint-condition Aston Martin Vanquish, retail value $228,000, that does zero to one hundred in ten seconds flat.

The hired help is a plus, the butlers and maids and chauffeurs and chefs and masseurs whose job depends on keeping Kane happy and ensuring he never lifts a finger for himself. And the women . . . he has to admit, the women are a big part of it, the internationally renowned beauties, the starlets, the heiresses, the modern-day Helens of Troy who fall at his feet and beg for his attention, who primp and pamper him and, when he gets bored, go gentle into that good night without so much as a wrinkle-inducing pout.

It is all that—but it is also more.

It is the power. It is knowing he can pick up the phone, or merely nod his head, and he can redeem a life—or destroy it. He commands legions. He is loved by the masses.

He is feared.

Kane threw his phone against the wall. It made contact with a loud *crack*, then clattered to the floor, a shattered piece of casing sliding under the couch. He had a plan. He knew the way his life was going to unfold; his every action was coolly calculated to bring him one step closer to the goal. *Stay cool,* that was the key. Cold, rational, disengaged. Keep emotions out of it. Stand on the sidelines, observe, interfere only when necessary, and only when the outcome is guaranteed.

Never, ever get involved.

These were rules he lived by, and they had their purpose.

He needed to protect himself if he was going to get what he wanted—and he *was* going to get it. What else mattered in life, if not that?

Something else. A whisper in his ear. *Something more.* He brushed it away.

The impulse to help, to save, to sacrifice, it was childish, he told himself. Immature. *Do the right thing*—it was a joke. Right and wrong were relative. *He* was the constant.

The plan was the constant. He had to think long-term. He had to forget Miranda and keep his eye on the ball.

"Keep your eye on the ball," Adam tells the fan, a seven-year-old who gazes at him with adoring eyes. The kid's shirt reads: I WANT TO SLAM LIKE ADAM. And you can tell from the look on his face that he does—he wants to do everything like Adam. Just like the rest of the country. His face on the cereal boxes, his name on the sneakers, his jersey in the hall of fame, and a championship ring on his finger—it's because he's the best, not just on the court, but off.

"Keep your eye on the ball," he says again, "that's all it takes."

The kid nods eagerly. Adam signs his basketball and moves on.

"The Humble Hero," they call him on TV, not because of his three-pointers, but because of the way he rescued that woman from a burning car and saved that child from drowning in a lake. He has paid for a young girl's heart transplant and endowed a home-less shelter. He does what he can, saves who he can, and asks nothing in return. The sports writers love him for loving the game. The talk show hosts love him for loving the world. The fans love him for being Adam Morgan, star athlete and model human being, selfless and charitable. Heroic.

They love him without knowing him, without needing to know him.

But back home, there is someone who does know him— someone who loves him not because he's good, but because she can't help it. She doesn't need his charity. She doesn't need his help, or his advice, or his endorsement. She doesn't need to be saved.

She just needs him.

Adam closed the blinds and stepped away from the window. Maybe Kane was right, and he had a hero complex. But what was so wrong with that? What was wrong with not wanting to be selfish? With wanting to fulfill his obligations?

He lay down on the bed, staring up at the ceiling. There was, of course, one very obvious thing wrong with it. He was miserable.

Not that he would have admitted it out loud. But alone, in his room, the window overlooking Harper's bedroom on one side, and the official offer from UC Riverside on the other, he finally had to face facts.

This sucked. She was probably over there right now hooking up with some other guy, and he was thirty feet away, struggling not to be selfish and not to make the wrong choices.

And, because it couldn't be said enough, he was alone.

They like me, they really like me, *she thinks, alone in the spotlight, a model for the masses. The master of ceremony unveils the plaque, and it is official: She is the newest member of the Haven High Hall of Fame.*

"Beth Manning was a model high school student who has grown into a model adult," says one of her former teachers.

"We're all so proud to have produced such an amazing alumna," says another. "I wish we could take the credit, but she was a lovely, kind-hearted, brave, brilliant, perfect student from the day she walked into the building right through the day she walked out."

"I want to be just like you when I grow up," one of the students tells her. "I mean, you're like Mother Teresa—you know, with better hair."

The love of her life is watching from the front row, his movie-star eyes filled with admiration. "Was my speech okay?" she whispers as she sits down next to him.

"It was brilliant." He kisses her. "You're brilliant. Everything you do amazes me."

"How can you say that," she asks, "when you know who I really am?"

"I can say that because I know who you really are," he tells her. He gazes at her, his dark, unruly hair flopping down over his

eyes. She pushes it out of the way for him, and he grabs her hand. There are black flecks of grease under his fingernails. "I know everything about you," he says, his voice warm and hoarse, a little scratchy, like he has just rolled out of bed. "And I love it all. The good and the bad. I love you." He takes her shoulders and turns her around to face the cheering crowd. "Everyone does."

Beth had always wanted to be liked. And she'd done everything she could to make it happen. She'd made the beds, done her homework, kissed her boyfriend, smiled at teachers, babysat her brothers, said please and thank you, bought on sale, arrived on time, looked before she leaped, followed the rules. Almost always followed the rules.

It hadn't worked.

Then she'd broken the rules, and that hadn't worked either.

She couldn't stop hearing Ashley Statten's cold voice: "I don't see how you're going to stop me." It was almost a dare.

No one liked her. And maybe it was time she stop caring. Maybe it was time she ignored the rules, and what people thought, and even what *she* wanted. Maybe getting people to like you was actually beside the point.

Harper, for one, was never going to like her. And the feeling was mutual. She'd get no credit for sabotaging the article, no credit for saving Harper from public humiliation. If she did it right, no one would ever know. But maybe she had a better reason to want to help. Maybe she had a responsibility. Maybe she needed to prove to herself—not to her teachers, not to her friends, not to the boy who was never going to look at her again with anything but disgust, but to herself—that she could stand up for something, for someone, even if it was hard, or especially then.

Maybe she just had nothing left to lose.

"Nothing to lose, baby!" Reed shouts, and dives off the stage, splashing into a sea of arms. He lies on his back as the fans hand him off, struggling to touch his shirt, to feel his arm, to grab a lock of his hair, a piece of the legacy, a touch, a taste, a whiff, anything, of a rock god.

They float him back to the stage and he leaps up, grabs his guitar, and plunges into the sound, and behind him the band rocks out and he sings. He sings that song they've been waiting to hear and the sound of their cries drowns out the music, but it's music to him, because they're the ones who make all this possible—the Top 40 singles, the platinum records, the Music Video Awards, the cover of Rolling Stone, *the mansions, the recording studio, the movie deals, the Fender Strat in his hand and the groupies waiting backstage—the sex, the drugs, the rock-'n'-roll.*

He loses himself in the music because he's got nothing to lose—he is *the music, it's all he cares about, all he loves. There's no one to let him down, no cares, no pain, only him, on his own, with his guitar, his voice, his songs, and his music. It's the only way to live.*

Reed slammed his hand down on the strings. What was the point in rehearsing? He was playing like shit. And he knew why. He couldn't stop thinking. He couldn't stop worrying, and wondering, and hating her, and missing her.

He just wanted to forget.

He'd tried alcohol. He'd tried pot. And now he'd

finally, after too many weeks of avoiding it, tried his guitar. They were all useless.

"Just stop!" he shouted, pressing his hands against his head like he could squeeze his brains out through his ears. That would be the dream. Nirvana. To finally stop thinking, stop *hurting*. He closed his eyes, willing it to all go away, disappear into a blinding white emptiness, to leave him with the ultimate dream, an empty mind.

A peaceful fog.

A merciful haze.

A blank.

She is . . .

She has . . .

She wants . . .

Nothing. Blank.

Miranda lay on her side, huddled up on the thin mattress, staring at the metal door—there were no bars, it turned out, but plenty of locks—that separated her from the outside world. And, because it hurt her too much to think about how she'd ended up there, she tried to think about where she was going.

She drew a blank.

Oh, she could mouth generic sentiments all day and all night, she knew all the right things to say, to paint a picture of her very bright future. She knew what she was *supposed* to want—the job, the husband, the kids, the oh-so-wonderful life—but when it came to what she actually wanted, she was clueless.

Who had time to think about that? There had always

been something else to do. Take care of her sister; obey her mother. Tend to Harper and solve the latest melodrama; chase after Kane. Miranda knew what her best friend wanted—she could write a book on the subject, and it would be a long one, given the hours she'd spent nursing Harper through every down, celebrating every up, analyzing to death every everything. And she'd tried to figure out what Kane wanted—tried to be the perfect girlfriend, sweet yet witty, undemanding, understanding. She'd spent years trying to catch him, and once she had, all she could think about was pleasing him. And look how far that had gotten her.

It was two nights before her high school graduation, and while the rest of the world was celebrating their bright and shining future, she was alone in a jail cell staring at a blank wall and a dead end. She felt empty, like she'd given everything she had to everyone else. And now that it was just herself, she had nothing left.

chapter

11

Beth wrapped the T-shirt around her fist. She stared at the window, gathering her courage. There were no lights behind the building, so all she could see was the narrow tunnel illuminated by her flashlight beam.

What if there's an alarm? she asked herself, her inner voice tight and panicky. These days, her inner voice lived in a constant state of panic, and she was tired of listening to it. She took a deep breath, drew back her fist, and punched the glass as hard as she could.

It bounced off with a dull thud.

Hysteria swept in, and Beth began to laugh. It always worked in the movies. A single punch, a satisfying crack, shards of glass exploding inward, and then, her hand protected by the T-shirt padding, would reach in and unlock the window, lift it up, climb through.

She punched the window again, kicked it twice, then sat down on the ground. Defeated.

She'd overcome her nerve, her nature, and her last

vestiges of common sense—only to be defeated by Plexiglas. All hail the wonders of the modern world.

"Am I interrupting something?"

She nearly screamed when she heard the voice, then again when she recognized it. And she couldn't help but wonder whether this was all a dream. Didn't it seem more likely that, after trying her best to find a solution to the Ashley Statten problem, she'd just given up—like always—and gone to bed? That now she was dreaming a life where she played the action hero—albeit a failed one?

It seemed a more logical explanation. Because what was realistic about Beth Manning sneaking out in the middle of the night to break into the *Journal*'s offices . . . and what made sense about Reed Sawyer showing up to watch her do it?

"What are you doing here?" she asked, turning around to face him. It was too dark to see anything but the dim outline of his figure, and though she had the flashlight, she chose not to turn it on. It seemed better to do this, whatever this was going to be, in the dark.

"What are *you* doing here?"

"I'm, uh . . ." She had prepared an elaborate excuse for herself, just in case she got caught, something about leaving her driver's license in the newsroom and needing to get it before the next day so she could drive her ailing grandmother to a doctor's appointment—but she'd lied to Reed enough. It was dark, it was late, she had failed, and—except at the end, when he'd walked away—Reed had always been the one person who hadn't judged her. He wouldn't turn her in. He probably wouldn't even care. "I'm breaking into the newspaper office." She sighed. "Or at least, I was trying to. Turns out breaking and entering is harder than it looks."

"Oh."

She waited for him to ask why.

"You want help?"

Beth flicked on the flashlight. She needed to know if he was mocking her. He squinted in the sudden light—but there was no smile on his face.

"Don't you want to know *why* I'm breaking in?" she asked.

"Is it a good reason?"

"I think so."

"Then no." He jerked his head toward the back door, then started toward it, pausing only to turn back and ask, "You want my help or not?"

She hurried after him. He pulled something out of his pocket and started fiddling with the doorknob.

"You know how to pick locks?" she asked incredulously.

He shrugged. "Not so tough."

Before she could ask *how* he knew, or *why*, they were inside. She hesitated in the doorway.

"Why are you here?" she asked him.

And maybe because she had told him the truth, or because it was even darker in the newsroom than it had been outside and he didn't have to see her face, he told the truth too. Or at least, what sounded like the truth. "I needed to see you," he said. "So I drove over to your house—but then I couldn't. So I just sat there. And when you drove away . . ."

"You followed me."

"Pretty much."

"Oh."

"You want to know why?" he asked.

She was afraid to say yes.

"I should probably do this and get out of here," she said quickly, turning the flashlight on again and heading for Ashley Statten's desk.

"So what are we doing?"

"Reed . . ." It was comforting to have him there—but that wasn't good enough. "You should go. I don't want to get you in trouble."

He shook his head. "I'm not leaving you alone here. So I can stand here and watch . . . or I can help."

So Beth gave him the flashlight and had him go through the drawers searching for Ashley's notes and hard copies, while she broke into the computer system—which, fortunately, didn't require anything more than finding the password taped to the inside of Ashley's top desk drawer—and deleted all traces of the article. Then she found the right camera, pulled its memory card, and deleted the incriminating photos.

"I think we got it—"

"Shhh!" Reed froze, and flicked off the flashlight beam.

Beth trembled in the dark as someone fumbled with a set of keys just outside the front door.

"Run!" Reed whispered. They took off for the back exit.

But the front door swung open too quickly. Beth dropped down behind a desk, holding her breath. She heard heavy footsteps, and the room burst into light—and then a deep, angry voice boomed out. "Stop!"

Caught. She knew she should be panicking or terrified, or at least in tears, but she was just calm. It was all over now. And there was a silver lining: At least she'd had time to destroy the article. Whatever trouble she got into, it would be worth it.

Beth gritted her teeth and prepared to stand up, when—

"You! Stop! Are there more of you?"

Reed's answer was calm and matter-of-fact, like he did this kind of thing every day. "No. It's just me."

"Dad, we need to talk."

Kane's father dropped his briefcase in surprise. "Why are you sitting in the dark?"

Kane didn't have an answer. His father snapped on the light.

"Working late again?" Kane asked sardonically. The only thing his father worked on past closing-time was his secretary.

"You know it." His father grinned and offered him a palm to slap; Kane declined.

"Something happened," Kane said. "I need your help."

"Hold on, not until I help myself." His father, as usual, veered straight for the liquor cabinet and poured himself a glass of scotch. He offered the bottle to Kane, who shook his head.

"Not tonight."

His father raised an eyebrow and took a sip, then sat down across from Kane. It was the same spot Harper had occupied a few hours before. "Girl trouble?"

"Not exactly." Kane leaned forward. "It's Miranda—

you've met her, I think. We've been, you know. A few weeks now."

His father chuckled. "Sounds like girl trouble to me." He leaned over and slapped Kane's knee. "It's about time, too—it's been a long time since you've needed any of the old Geary wisdom. So what's the deal with this girl? Is she hot?" He laughed again. "Look who I'm asking—of course she's hot."

"I don't need your . . . wisdom," Kane said, trying to suppress his irritation with the aging-playboy act. "I need your lawyer."

Kane's father sank back into the couch, the smirk wiped off his face. "What did you do?"

What did *I do*? Kane asked himself, but didn't wait for the answer. That was a completely separate issue; the problem now was helping Miranda. And Kane had to believe that whatever he had or hadn't done was irrelevant.

"The cops pulled us over for speeding and found a stash in her car," Kane said. "Just pot, nothing big, but you know these cops—"

"All too well," his father said, scowling, and there was a pause long enough for them both to remember the time Kane had narrowly escaped prosecution for his fake ID business—escaped only because his father's skills in bribery and blackmail rivaled his own.

"They're not going to let it go, and her mother's being a total bitch about the whole thing, and if she gets stuck with some incompetent public defender . . ." He refused to think about it. "Can you just hook me up with your lawyer? I can pay you back, eventually." Although now that his prospective cash flow had dried up—half his product was impounded at the Grace police station, and the rest of it wouldn't be seeing the light of day for a long, long time—he didn't know how.

"You want me to lend you *my* money and *my* lawyer so you can get your deadbeat girlfriend out of jail?" his father asked incredulously. "And in this fantasy world where I enable your juvenile delinquency, am I offering bail money, too?"

"You don't have to be such an asshole about it," Kane said, trying not to get angry, and failing. "She's not a juvenile delinquent."

"No, just a drug dealer," he said snidely. "And an incompetent one at that. When are you going to learn that you have to stop hanging around with people like this, son? Surrounding yourself with bad influences. It's idiotic. You're better than that—you've got a future ahead of you."

"What if I were to tell you that *I* was the bad influence, and that I was the one—"

"I'm going to stop you right there, son, because in the hypothetical I think you're about to propose, you'd find yourself with a criminal record, probably a felony, and there's nothing I could do about that, lawyer or not. That means no Penn State, no future, no nothing."

They stared at each other, and Kane knew that his father knew. Knew and was willing to stay silent, as long as Kane played along. Kane looked away first. "That's why I need to help her," he said quietly.

"And I'm your father, which is why I need to help you. And the best way to do that is keeping you as far away from this mess as possible. This girl's not your responsibility—I see no reason for you to get involved."

"What's wrong with you?"

"I'm your father," he said. "I'm just trying to do what's best."

"You're choosing *now* to be a parent?" Kane asked, outraged. "After everything?" After all the late nights, and the girls, and the drinking, and the lessons in manipulation and emotional blackmail, after all the buddy-buddy midnight oversharing his father had forced in a pathetic effort to pretend he was still eighteen? After leaving Kane and his brother to raise themselves, forgetting to stock the refrigerator or enroll them in school or do any of the things any normal parent would file under "what's best," he was choosing *now* to pull a Father Knows Best and lay down the law?

"Don't give me that weepy bullshit!" his father shouted. He stood, too. He was still several inches taller than Kane. "You know I did the best I could for you boys. After your mother—" He slammed down the glass of scotch. "I did everything I could."

"Yeah, you were a stellar parent," Kane drawled. "Father of the year."

"I gave you what you needed," his father said coldly. "I taught you boys what matters in life. I taught you how to look out for yourself. That's all you need."

"Lucky for me," Kane said. "Because that's all I got."

Miranda had never understood claustrophobia. Until now. Now she got it, the way the air hung heavy and the walls closed in, the thoughts battered her brain—*What if there's a fire? What if the ceiling collapses? What if? What if?*—worst-case scenarios of doom and destruction through which she would suffer alone, trapped by four windowless walls and one padlocked door.

So when the key turned in the lock and the door swung open, her heart sang. And even though they weren't there to set her free, or tell her that her mother had decided to love her after all, but only to march her down a hallway and into yet another dark, closet-size, locked room, even then she felt a little bit better.

Because sitting across from her, his hands folded on top of a thin manila file and his face composed into a rigid smile of professional competence and faint empathy, was a lawyer. And that meant hope.

Her escort didn't handcuff her to a chair or stand guard with his gun drawn. He just sat her down and walked out, closing the door behind him, and Miranda could, if she really tried, savor the illusion that she was in some other little room, far away, having a polite chat with a pleasant stranger. At least until the lawyer opened his mouth and launched into a litany of terrifying terms—sentence, felony, misdemeanor, arraignment, circumstantial, worst-case scenario—pausing occasionally to wipe his runny nose on a soggy handkerchief, the same handkerchief he used not once, but twice, to wipe away imaginary smudges on his horn-rimmed glasses.

And then, all too quickly, he was standing up and shaking her hand, and telling her he'd see her in the morning.

"But you just got here," she protested. "Aren't you going to get me out? What about bail? I can find someone to—"

"I thought they'd already explained all that to you," he said, sniffing. "We can't even start on the bail process until the morning, and then there's the question of arraignment, and getting onto the docket, and I think the judge is out with some kind of"—he sneezed—"bronchial infection."

Miranda knew it was irrational, but she couldn't let him leave, not until he'd promised her that he could fix this. "Look, I didn't do anything. You're going to help me prove that, right? Please?" She knew she sounded pathetic, but at this point, she didn't much care.

The lawyer slid the file into his pleather briefcase with a sigh. "Melissa—"

"Miranda."

"Of course, of course. I can't make you any promises, but no one wants to go to court on something petty like this. It's a waste of everyone's time. I'm sure we can plea them down to a few misdemeanor charges, some community service—"

"Are you not listening to me?" Tears of anger spurted out of the corners of her eyes. "I didn't *do* anything. I can't let people think I'm a drug dealer, I can't have that on my record. You have to *fix this*."

"Melinda—"

"Miranda."

"It's late," he said, flicking his eyes toward his watch. "I only came by because they said you were having a meltdown. I just wanted to run through the basics with you. We'll talk more tomorrow. I promise."

"I'm screwed, aren't I?" she said, not meaning to whisper but unable to muster enough air to speak in a normal voice.

The lawyer gave two sharp raps on the door, and it swung open at his command.

"We'll talk tomorrow," he said again. "I'm sure we'll figure something out. Trust me."

Miranda just hung her head and let the cop waiting outside escort her back to her room. Her cell. She was done trusting people. It was a mistake. Why else was she here?

You know why you're here.

She sat down on her cot, wide awake, willing the door to magically swing open and set her free. But it stayed closed, trapping her with her thoughts.

It's your own fault.

She hadn't trusted too much. That would have been understandable; that would have been forgivable. Miranda picked up the thin, lumpy pillow and squeezed it between her hands. *Trusting* would imply that she had been naïve, that she had been deceived.

But that wasn't it at all. She'd known exactly who Kane was, *what* he was. And she had allowed it. She had never demanded he be anything more than the selfish, self-centered, arrogant jerk he'd proven himself to be, time and time again. She'd let Kane be Kane, and she just went along for the ride, afraid to ask for anything more.

That wasn't blind trust. It was just stupidity.

She punched the pillow, and then, because it didn't make a good thud and it didn't hurt, she punched the wall. Hard. Pain shot through her knuckles and up her arm.

She had let this happen to her. Just like she let *everything* happen to her.

She let her mother push her around, call her an ungrateful daughter, berate her, insult her, and then demand that Miranda be available to her every beck and call.

She let Harper lean on her, interrupt her life with melodramas sometimes tragic and sometimes petty, cry on her shoulder—and she let Harper push her around, and use her, abuse her, and basically do whatever she wanted without thought or concern about how Miranda would feel.

Miranda stayed silent, because what if she spoke up and asked something for herself and the answer was no? What if they left her one by one, because they found out who she really was—fat and ugly and boring and needy? What if she ended up alone? She'd let the what-ifs eat her up inside, and instead of standing up for herself stayed quiet, tended to other people's needs—and, whenever it got to be too much, locked herself in the bathroom and threw it all up.

Because, sooner or later, some things just need to come out.

She disgusted herself.

She punched the wall again, and again—then stopped abruptly, bringing her fist to her mouth, sucking on her stinging knuckles.

Enough.

Enough hating herself. Enough *hurting* herself. Enough swallowing other people's shit with a happy smile. Enough keeping quiet. Enough fear.

When she got out—and she *would* get out, she told herself, one way or another, she would ensure that Kane didn't get a chance to ruin her life—things would change. *She* would change. She would fight. She would move out of the house, whatever her mother said. Figure out what she wanted—and get it.

She would start a new life.

And this one would be her own.

"You want to tell me what you're doing here?" the man asked. From where she was crouching, Beth could only see his shoes. But she recognized the voice: It was the editor in chief.

Reed didn't say anything.

"I could have just had the cops come check this out, you know," the editor said. "But I wanted to see for myself who was trying to break into my newsroom."

Reed still didn't speak.

"So you're going to answer me, kid." The editor got louder. "And tell me what you're doing here. *Now.*"

There was a long silence.

"Fine, then. I'm calling the cops. Enjoy prison."

Beth didn't let herself stop to think, because if she had, she might have chickened out; or her legs, already weak and quivering, might have rebelled and refused to stand. So without thinking, she stood and revealed herself. "Don't call the cops," she pleaded, squinting in the bright light. "Please."

The editor in chief gaped at her. He was gripping a baseball bat. "Aren't you the new intern? What the hell are you doing here?"

She could have made up an excuse, but he was going to find out eventually. "I broke in and erased Ashley's article," she admitted. "It was a personal attack on . . . a friend of mine, and I—I know it was wrong, but I had to. Reed—" She winced, realizing she should never have said his name. "He had nothing to do with it. He found me here, and he was just trying to stop me, I swear."

Reed looked at her like she was crazy.

Don't say anything, she pleaded with him silently, hoping he could still read her eyes. *Just shut up and let me do this for you.*

The editor shook his head in disbelief and, with a long sigh, put down the bat. "You broke into my newsroom to destroy one of my stories? I suppose you're expecting me to compliment you on your moxie or something?"

Beth just pressed her lips together and waited.

"That's not how things work in the real world, young lady." He took off his glasses and rubbed his eyes. "But your teacher thinks you walk on water—and while she's obviously wrong about that, I don't want to humiliate her by getting you arrested. Which doesn't mean there won't be consequences."

"If you have to call the police, please just let Reed get out of here first," Beth pleaded. "I swear, he's not involved. He was only here to talk me out of this. Please."

"You're not really in a position to be asking for anything right now," the editor said sternly. "But . . . I'm not calling the cops."

Beth felt all the adrenaline leak out of her body. As the crisis moment passed, the fear returned.

But something else came with it: pride. Because this time, she hadn't given in to the fear. She'd done what she needed to do, and that had to count for something.

"You're fired, obviously," the editor snapped. "And I'll be informing your school about this. And your parents. We'll let them decide how to deal with it."

"Thank you," Beth said, surprised to discover she wasn't crying. "Thank you so much."

"Don't thank me, just get out." He looked down—and

Beth realized that beneath his long coat he was wearing pajama pants. "I'm going home to bed."

Beth and Reed, without looking at each other or speaking, filed out of the office. The editor locked up behind them, glared at Beth for a long moment, then stalked away.

"Thanks," Reed said quietly. "You could've just stayed down and kept your mouth shut. So . . . thanks."

"I couldn't let you take the blame."

"You could have," he said. "You just didn't."

They walked down the dark street together. Beth's car was parked a block away, and Reed's was just behind it.

"I followed you because I was worried," he said suddenly.

"What?"

"Tonight. When you left. I thought—I don't know. It was late and it seemed like . . . something was wrong. I just knew."

They paused on the sidewalk between their two cars.

"You were worried about me?" Beth asked, not sure what she was supposed to think.

Reed laughed; she'd missed the sound of his laugh, warm and scratchy at the same time, like a wool blanket that had been in the attic for too long. "Crazy, right? What kind of trouble could you be getting into?"

She smiled up at him, and though she was sure it was too dark for him to see, he reached out his hand and almost touched her cheek. His arm fell away just before it made contact. "You don't smile enough. Anymore."

"I didn't know you were watching."

Reed shrugged.

"I'm not back together with Adam," she said, then felt stupid, suddenly feeling like she'd said exactly the wrong thing. "I mean, I know you don't care, it doesn't matter, I just thought . . . I wanted you to know. We're not together."

"Okay."

They watched each other, and she thought how strange it was to look at someone's eyes without looking away, how it made you feel so connected to the other person and disconnected from everything else, all at the same time.

"So . . . ," he finally said, still staring at her.

"So . . . I should probably, um . . ."

"Beth—" He raised his hands and cupped her chin, so gently, and she leaned forward and for a moment she thought, no, she *knew* it was all going to be okay, the world was somehow going to give her all the things she wanted but didn't deserve, Reed had finally found a way to forgive her, he still loved her, she could see it in his eyes, how much he wanted to go back to what they used to have— and then he bent her face forward and kissed her softly on the forehead. "Good night."

chapter

12

She didn't get it. And she certainly didn't believe it. Not at first. Not when the cop opened the door to her cell and escorted her out—not, this time, with a grip firmly clamped around her arm, but with a smile, and a small wave of the hand to indicate she should follow behind. Not when they brought her to a counter marked PROPERTY and gave her back her watch and her purse. Not even when she followed the cop into the lobby and he nodded toward the door and said, once again, "You're free to go."

Miranda just stared at him. "I don't understand. What happened?"

The cop smiled implacably, though only the lower half of his face moved. His stare stayed cool and emotionless. "I can't discuss details of a current investigation."

"But it's an investigation of *me!*" she protested.

The cop shook his head. "Not anymore."

And that's when she saw him, heading down the hall in a familiar direction, toward the doors that locked only from the outside. His fingertips were smudged with black ink.

"Kane?" she said wonderingly. "Kane!"

The woman guiding him down the hall—Carrie, the same one who'd shepherded her around the night before—paused and looked back at her. But Kane just stared down the floor as if he hadn't heard.

Miranda followed him with her eyes, expecting to feel some stab of sympathy—after all, she knew where he was headed, and what he was facing. But she felt nothing. Not even curiosity about what had happened, how he had ended up in the dark, narrow hallway while she faced an open door.

He wasn't her concern, not anymore. She had to focus on herself.

And on that front, it seemed, things were starting to look up.

Miranda tested out a smile, and although the cop didn't react, it felt good on her face. "I can really leave? Just . . . go? You believe me, that I didn't do anything? This is over?"

The cop nodded. "Everything's been cleared up. Sorry for your trouble." He didn't sound sorry; Miranda didn't much care. She was out of there, out of danger, and suddenly everything seemed lighter, brighter—*easier*. All the vows she'd made to herself the night before, lying in the darkness, desperately hoping she would have a chance to fulfill them, they all seemed ridiculously easy. What was facing down her mother or sticking up to Harper, compared to prison?

"I can leave," she murmured to herself, wanting to scream it out loud, wanting to sing. But she just walked quietly toward the door and, savoring the power, the *freedom* that came with the simple gesture, opened it.

"Miranda, wait!" a woman called.

For a moment, Miranda was tempted to run. Her heart slamming, she knew, deep down, that a mistake had been made and the woman had arrived to correct it, to drag her back inside, into the dark, lonely, locked cell—that unless she fled, far and fast, she might never get her chance to leave again.

"I have something for you," the woman said. It was Carrie, and she was smiling—this was a real smile, one that crinkled the corners of her eyes and made them sparkle. "From your boyfriend—"

"He's not my boyfriend," Miranda snapped, and saying it out loud wasn't nearly as painful as she'd expected it to be.

"Oh. Well. Anyway, he left you this." She held out a piece of paper, folded over a few times into the size of a playing card. Miranda recognized the familiar scrawl covering both sides of the page.

She didn't want to know what he had to say for himself, but she took the note and slipped it into her back pocket. "Thanks."

"He turned himself in, you know," Carrie said.

Too little, too late, Miranda thought bitterly. She pressed her lips together and gave Carrie a tight nod. "They said I can go now."

"Of course you can—and make sure you have a great day!" Carrie said in a chirpy voice that matched neither the situation nor the setting.

Miranda grinned back and did her best to muster equal levels of perkiness. She could feel the note bulging in her pocket, but it didn't matter; it was already part of the past.

"Thanks," she said again, meaning it this time. Her smile grew wider as she grasped the doorknob and, once again, pushed the door open, this time stepping through without looking back. "I think I will."

Haven High loved scandals and hated Beth, which meant word of her criminal trespasses made the rounds at lightning speed. By the time Adam woke up the next morning, he had six voice mails and four text messages gleefully alerting him to the second-best gossip of the night. He didn't even get out of bed before reaching for the phone.

"Are you okay?" he asked as soon as she'd picked up.

"I'm fine," Beth said, sounding strange. Not like she was lying, though. And maybe that was the strange part—she really did sound fine.

Adam sat up in bed, tossing back the covers. His bedroom faced southeast, and by midmorning this time of year, it was boiling. "Is it true? You broke into—"

"I don't really want to talk about it," she said, without emotion.

"Right. Okay. But . . . are you in trouble?"

He could hear her sigh.

"Well, I'm grounded until forever," she said lightly. He knew it was the first time she'd ever been grounded, or, as far as he knew, punished at all. "But I don't think the school can get me into much trouble. What are they going to do, suspend me?"

"Was that a *joke*?" he asked incredulously. Graduation was only a day away; soon the entire senior class would be suspended. Permanently.

"Not a very good one, but I guess so. Why? You don't think I have a sense of humor?"

"No, I just thought . . ."

"You thought I'd be curled up in bed weeping, wondering how I was going to go on?" she suggested. "Or maybe you thought I had some kind of breakdown last night and went psycho, what with the whole breaking-and-entering thing?"

"Well . . ." He laughed a little. "Sort of. So . . . you want me to come over or anything? Keep you company?"

There was a pause. "Do you *want* to come over?"

"I will, no big deal," he said, though he'd had other plans for the day. Well, not plans, not quite, but something he wanted to do, or at least wanted to think about doing, something that could have been important. Something for himself. "If you need me to."

"Try again, Ad. Do you *want* to? Honest answer."

He hesitated. Just because she said she wanted his honest answer didn't mean it was true. Did he owe her the lie? Or did he owe her the truth?

"I didn't think so," she said, before he could answer. "And I don't need you to. I don't need you to feel sorry for me anymore, Ad, or to stick by me because you think I can't deal on my own."

"I told you, that's not—"

"I know, I know," she said quickly. "It's not the only reason, but it's *a* reason, you said it yourself. Don't lie now."

Who *was* this girl, the one who sounded so much like the Beth he used to know, calm and confident and in control?

"What do you want me to say?"

"Nothing. You don't owe me anything anymore. We're friends. You've been an amazing friend, Ad, but you don't have to . . . you don't have to worry about me. Not anymore. I'm okay. Or I'm going to be. I should have been okay a long time ago, but . . . better late than never, right?" She laughed nervously as he tried to figure out what she was talking about.

"Time's running out, Adam," she said. "Don't waste it on me."

"This isn't about—"

"It's always been about her," Beth cut in. "Even when we were together, everything was always about her."

"No," he protested.

"It doesn't matter anymore," Beth said. "That's over now."

"Beth—" There was too much he wanted to say, too many regrets about the things he'd done and the things he hadn't said and the way everything had ended up, completely screwed up and broken, so much pain that it seemed like, if he tried, he could trace it all back to one bad decision. His own.

"I loved you, too," she said quietly. "I hope she makes you happy. You deserve that."

Adam didn't know what he deserved, but as he hung up the phone, he knew that he had to stop asking himself the question. Just this once, he would go after what he wanted. She was less than a hundred feet away, maybe lying in bed thinking about him—maybe, though it made Adam sick to imagine it, she was thinking about Jake Oberman, or some other guy who'd managed to weasel his way in.

It didn't matter, he told himself. He'd wasted time, but

he had to believe he hadn't missed his chance. He just needed to find a way to persuade her. A big way, something so dramatic, so romantic, so unforgettable that she wouldn't be able to walk away again—something that would, in one stroke, overcome everything that had come between them this year, that would make her see the truth, and believe it: He wanted to be with her.

Only her.

He just hoped it wasn't too late.

Harper rushed over to Miranda's house as soon as she got the call, and when the door opened, she threw herself around Miranda and squeezed.

"Um, choking," Miranda gasped after a few moments.

"Shut up." Harper realized her face was wet with tears. She didn't care. Miranda was home safe, and that's all that mattered. "Are you okay? Tell me you're okay."

"Okay. But. Can't. Breathe," Miranda teased, trying to break free. Harper just squeezed tighter.

"If you think I'm ever letting go, you're crazy." She did let go, eventually, but only once she'd forced herself to stop crying. By the time Miranda saw her face, she wanted everything to look normal and casual. Not to mention happy. "What can I do? Do you want to go lie down? You must be tired. I could bring you some of your favorite foods, or we could watch one of those lame movies you like, or—"

"I'm not an invalid," Miranda protested. She glanced over her shoulder, a scowl darkening her face. "Let's just get out of here, okay? I don't want to be stuck in the house with *her*."

"Anything you want." Harper grabbed her arm and dragged her to the car. "Tell me everything. Unless you don't want to talk about it. Do you want to talk about it? Whatever you want, okay?"

Miranda just rolled her eyes and headed for the car—Harper's car, of course, since Miranda's was still impounded at the police station. "We can talk when we get to wherever we're going. Let's just . . . let's just relax and enjoy, okay?"

So they were mostly silent for the ride. Harper stuck in Miranda's favorite CD, a mix of Top 40 songs from the year they were in ninth grade, and drove toward what she promised Miranda would be "the perfect place."

"The *Fun Zone?*" Miranda asked incredulously, as the car pulled to a stop outside the garish pink and green building, its sign shouting its mission statement—FUN! FUN! FUN!—in six-feet tall neon. "You brought me to the Fun Zone?"

"We don't have to go in if you don't want to," Harper said, wondering if she'd done exactly the wrong thing. "I just thought . . . you know, you've been so into the nostalgia thing lately, and I don't know if you remember, but—"

"Of course I do." Miranda giggled. "Remember when we hid ourselves under those little colored balls and your mom thought we'd disappeared?"

Harper burst into laughter. "She almost had a heart attack, and she kept yelling that someone needed to—" She cut herself off. It didn't seem so funny anymore.

"To call the cops," Miranda finished for her. "It's okay, really."

"I thought I'd be grounded forever after that one," Harper said ruefully.

"It felt like forever," Miranda said. "A month is a long time when you're nine years old."

For years, the Fun Zone had been their birthday tradition. It was a dark, noisy zoo filled with video games, rides, cheap pizza, and screaming kids: every parent's nightmare and every child's dream. Harper and Miranda had only been allowed there on special occasions and so, twice a year, for each of their birthdays, they'd made the pilgrimage to kiddie nirvana, slapping quarters into slots, pushing joysticks until their thumbs cramped, stuffing themselves with pizza and cotton candy and, always, toasting each other with chocolate milk shakes and pledging that they would be best friends forever.

The tradition had died out sometime around age twelve, when suddenly nothing without shopping or cute boys or makeup had qualified as much of a fun zone. At least for Harper. Miranda had always talked of the place fondly, while Harper mainly remembered it as a greasy stink-pit of sweat and noise. But this was Miranda's day. Harper had turned off her phone, cancelled her plans, and was ready for some serious girl-on-girl bonding.

"This is perfect," Miranda said, beaming. "Let's do it."

The Fun Zone wasn't that crowded, and they were able to find a table where they ordered their regular pepperoni pizza and, of course, two chocolate milk shakes. Harper half expected Miranda to object to the milk shakes and steeled herself not to comment, not today. Today Miranda could eat—or not eat—whatever she wanted. But Miranda just smiled and let the waitress walk away.

"Place hasn't changed much," Miranda observed as a

screaming seven-year-old ran past her chair, his younger sister hot on his tail.

"Fun, fun, fun!" Harper said sarcastically as they both ducked a water gun spray.

"Okay, so it's not quite heaven on earth anymore," Miranda admitted. "But it's good. Thanks for thinking of it. And for, you know, being here."

Harper wanted to grab her and hug her again, but she held herself back. "I wouldn't be anywhere else, Rand," she said, more seriously than she'd ever said anything in the Fun Zone. "I hope you know that."

Miranda nodded. The waitresses returned with their milk shakes, and Harper lifted hers in the air. "To you," she suggested.

"It's bad luck to drink to yourself," Miranda protested. "Besides, we should stick to our old toast, don't you think? It's tradition."

"We're not ten anymore—" Harper began, then caught the look on Miranda's face and shut herself up. "Okay." She struggled to remember the familiar litany. "To you and me, best friends forever, until hell freezes over—"

"Until pigs fly," Miranda chimed in.

"Until Niagara Falls."

"To infinity and beyond."

Harper hesitated before the traditional last line, then smiled and clinked her glass against Miranda's. "Till death do us part."

They played a few of the arcade games and even tested out the ball cage—before getting tossed out for being over the age limit—but eventually had to admit to themselves that some things just aren't so much fun anymore once you're all grown up. (Although Miranda *did* enjoy beating Harper on the retro Ms. Pac-Man machine, a feat she'd never managed to accomplish as a kid.) All too soon, they found themselves back at the table, picking over their pizza crusts and ordering a second round of milk shakes.

Harper propped her elbows on the table and gave Miranda the Stare. "Okay. Tell me. Are you okay? Do you want to talk about it?"

Miranda closed her eyes and for a second she was back there in that cell, and she *did* want to talk about it, but suddenly she couldn't get the words out. Her throat closed up, her eyes teared, and, beneath the table, her knees began to tremble. And maybe it was better not to push it. Why wallow in bad memories? It seemed self-indulgent and depressing, especially since Harper was trying so hard to cheer her up. She smiled, hoping it looked real. "I'm fine, I swear, it was no big deal. Sort of an adventure. I'm sick of thinking about the whole thing. What's going on with *you*?"

Harper wrinkled her nose. "Really?"

"Really. Any movement on the Jake Oberman front?"

Harper looked dubious but then shrugged, and launched into a typical Harper Grace monologue. "We were actually supposed to go out today, but I blew him off, and I have to admit, I'm not that sorry about it. I mean, I don't know, Rand, he's totally hot and all, and he seems like a nice guy, but . . ."

Miranda zoned out. She couldn't focus on Harper's love life, not when her own was . . . well, what love life?

That was over now, and she didn't want to feel sorry

about it, she wouldn't *let* herself feel sorry about it, but when she thought about Kane . . .

The letter was still in her pocket. She half wanted to read it, but she knew that once she did, she wouldn't be able to forget what it said. Whatever it said. There'd be no going back. So for now, it was still folded up. Untouched.

And Harper was still talking. *Nothing ever changes,* Miranda thought. *I go to jail, and she still can't shut up about herself for one minute—*

And whose fault is that?

"I'm not fine," she said suddenly.

Harper's mouth snapped shut. There was an audible *click* as her teeth banged together.

"I'm not fine, and it *was* a big deal," Miranda said, swallowing hard. She stared over Harper's shoulder at some kid who was rubbing chocolate cake all over his face. "It was horrible. I thought I was—I don't know. I just didn't think I was going to be able to handle it. And I thought I was going to prison or something, and it all just . . ." She wasn't crying, but she had that hollow, shivery feeling in her chest that told her it was only a matter of time, so she stopped talking and pressed her face between her hands, like she could somehow squeeze out all the bad thoughts.

"Thank god!" Harper exclaimed.

Miranda looked up at her in surprise.

"No, I don't mean thank god it was horrible," Harper said. She reached across the table and grabbed Miranda's hand. "I just mean thank god you want to talk about it. You were really freaking me out with all that 'I'm fine, I'm good, happy happy, joy joy' stuff. So what was it like?"

"You really want to know?"

"No, Rand," Harper said sarcastically. "I want you to sit here and listen to me talk about what I watched on TV last night, because that's oh so much more important."

Miranda took a deep breath. "Okay, well, the first thing is, it turns out I'm a little claustrophobic. . . ." And she told Harper everything, starting from how terrified and ashamed she'd been when the handcuffs went on, to the horror of being fingerprinted and searched, to the night she had spent alone in her cell, counting the panels in the ceiling and wondering how she would survive another hour, then another. And then there was the worst moment of all, the realization that Kane was to blame—and that he was leaving her there alone to face his consequences.

"That asshole," Harper said, hatred in her voice. "I still can't believe he did that to you. I could kill him."

"He did turn himself in," Miranda protested weakly.

Harper looked horrified. "Rand, please, *please* don't tell me you're thinking about forgiving him. Or that you actually feel sorry for him or something."

"No. *No.*" And she wasn't lying, she knew that. "I just . . . I don't hate him. Is that weird? I know I should probably hate him. Or miss him. Or something. But I'm just . . . I don't know. Numb."

"Maybe you're in shock," Harper suggested.

"Maybe. I kind of hope not." She shook herself as if she could fling away all the unpleasant memories that coated her skin like the scent of the jail cell, which three showers in a row hadn't managed to wash away. "So I guess I'm single again." She laughed softly, amazed she was able to find even a bitter humor in the situation. "Looks like we better get cable next year, since it seems like I'll be putting in some serious couch-time."

"Next year?" Harper said, leaning forward. "You mean . . . ?"

"I mean next year in our apartment," Miranda said, grinning. "If you're still looking for a roommate, that is."

Harper looked like she was going to explode. "Really? You're sure? We're getting out of here together?"

"As soon as humanly possible," Miranda confirmed. "And I promise, I'll try to keep the 'why, oh why am I single?' whining to a minimum."

"I wouldn't worry about that," Harper said, "since I'll be whining right along with you."

Miranda raised an eyebrow—at least she'd gained one useful skill from Kane. "What about Jake?"

"I don't think it's going to happen," Harper admitted. "I wish I could, but I'm just . . ."

"Not over Adam?"

Harper looked down and began playing with her straw, stirring the remnants of the milk shake round and round in the bottom of the glass. "I don't think he's the kind of thing you get over," she said finally. "But *it's* over. I get that now. And I think . . . I think I can be okay on my own."

Now Miranda was the one to reach across the table. "You're not on your own."

Harper squeezed her hand gratefully. "Aren't I the one who's supposed to be comforting you?"

"Given that you're just as screwed up as I am, I think this can be an equal-opportunity comfort session," Miranda teased.

"Hey, at least I'm not a felon!"

"That's ex-con, to you," Miranda corrected her. "So you don't want to mess with me."

"Ooh, are you going to shiv me or something?"

Miranda laughed. "Someone's been watching too many episodes of *Prison Break*."

"What else was I supposed to do?" Harper asked. "*Someone* wasn't available to play with, and life is somewhat dull when you're not around."

"Yes, I know, you can't live without me," Miranda teased.

"You're right." Harper grinned. "And since it's all about me, after all, thank god you're back."

Miranda raised her glass. "I'll drink to that."

Adam was sitting on her doorstep.

She almost missed him in the dark.

"Your phone's been off," he said, when she came in range.

"I was with Miranda." Harper tried not to betray her surprise. "Did you need something?"

"How is she?" he said. "Miranda."

Harper shrugged. "You know Miranda. She says she's okay, but . . ."

"If she's not, she will be," Adam said. "She's tough."

"Yeah . . . I hope so."

Adam dangled a piece of black fabric from his hand. "I need to blindfold you."

"You need to—what?" She took a closer look. "Is that a *sock*?"

Adam blushed. "It's the best I could do. It's clean."

"You want to blindfold me, and then . . . ?"

"It's a surprise." He stood up, brushed himself off, and came over to her, putting his hands on her shoulders. "Trust me?"

Harper couldn't stop the smile. "Always."

But she stopped him just as he was about to tie the long, black sock around her eyes. "You *sure* it's clean?"

He didn't answer, just tied it tight and then took her hand and led her through the darkness.

"Watch your head," he warned, guiding her into a car. His hands were warm and firm, one gripping her arm, the other flat on her lower back. She didn't want him to let go, but then he did, and a door slammed. Another opened, and she heard him get in next to her.

"I hope you're not expecting me to drive," she teased.

"I got it from here," Adam said, and started the car.

Harper hated surprises, as she hated anything out of her control. But she didn't ask any questions. She didn't want him to think she was actually enjoying this. So instead she sat quietly, listening to his breathing, which sounded very loud in the dark.

It was hard to keep track of the time when she had nothing to measure it by but the sound of his breathing, the gravel crunching under the tires, and the wind rushing past. But it didn't feel like very long before they had arrived.

Adam opened the door for her and guided her out, then put an arm around her waist and, with his other arm, took her hand in a strangely formal gesture. At first, she took tiny, hesitant steps, worrying that she would catch her heel on something and pitch face first into the ground. But the farther they walked, the more certain she became that Adam wouldn't let her fall.

Another door opened, and they were inside, her feet clicking on tile. The smell was familiar, but she couldn't place it, and she wasn't trying too hard. It was better to just coast on the warm, safe feeling of Adam's arms, because she knew that all too soon, he would let go. And then he did.

"Ready?" he asked.

More than ready. "You tell me."

"One more thing." He left her standing there alone, and it was disorienting, almost terrifying, standing in a strange place surrounded by darkness, not knowing who or what might be watching. So disorienting that she was about to rip the makeshift blindfold off herself, surprise or no surprise—and then the music started.

> *I belong in your eyes,*
> *I lose myself in you.*

It was a slow song, a love song.

> *With you I live,*
> *Without you I cry,*
> *Without you I die.*

Harper almost gasped. It was the song that had been playing at the prom, as she stood alone, waiting for her prince.

Adam slipped something onto her head, then took off her blindfold. The first thing she saw was his eyes, green and sparkling and misty soft. Then the dimple that appeared whenever he smiled. Next the cheesy cardboard crown on his head, painted gold and lined with sequins.

And, finally, she pulled her eyes away from him and realized they were in the school gym, surrounded by streamers, balloons, sparkling lights, and a fake Eiffel Tower.

"You did this?" she whispered. He nodded. "How—Adam, what's going on?"

He took a step closer, then another, and looped his arms around her waist. "I'll explain everything, but first, can we dance?"

And, despite her vow to protect herself, to forget about Adam, to move on, she put her arms around him, leaned her head against her shoulder, closed her eyes, and lost herself in his embrace.

"You made me the prom?" she murmured. They swayed gently with the music, barely lifting their feet off the ground.

"I got some friends in high places. Or at least, on prom committee."

"But why?" His shoulder was so soft, and, just like she remembered, she fit perfectly into the dip where it met his neck.

"I should have been here." Adam stroked her hair. "I wish I could go back. But . . ."

"But you can't."

"I thought maybe, just tonight, we could go back and pretend this whole year didn't happen—"

Harper stopped dancing and, though she hated to do so, pushed him away. "Adam, what is this, really? Because if this is just pretend, if you're just having one night of fun before—" She took a deep breath and drew herself up very straight, trying to make her voice as hard as possible. "What is this supposed to mean?"

Adam, who hated talking about—well, pretty much anything that didn't come with a scoreboard—didn't look away. "It means I want you, Harper. And not just for tonight."

"So what changed?" she asked, afraid to let herself believe him. "I suddenly *need* you more than Beth does? Did my spine disintegrate? Because I must have missed the memo."

Adam's hand grazed her cheek. She didn't push him away.

"I don't care if you need me," he said. "I need you. I *want* you. When you made me choose—"

"Maybe I shouldn't have," she admitted quietly, though it went against her principles to admit a mistake.

He shook his head. "Beth is my friend, she needed help. But you—"

"I never need help," Harper said bitterly. It was a tired old song, and by now she knew the words by heart. "I'm strong. I can stand up on my own. Blah blah blah."

He grabbed her hands in his. "I was going to say, you're more than a friend. You're my best friend. You always have been, Gracie. You're everything."

Harper sighed, still hearing Kane's words ringing in her ears.

We look out for ourselves
We take what we want.
We don't care who gets hurt.
We're the same.

"I don't need to be your whole world," she said, trying to convince herself as much as Adam. "I just . . . I need to matter. I need to know you're on my side, and I know you *say* you are, but it seems like there's always something else more important—"

"Harper, look at me."

As if she could look away.

His gaze was fierce, and his eyes too bright, as if covered by a sheen of tears. But that was impossible. This was Adam. "You matter," he said. "And there is *no one* else. I will always choose you. I need you. Do you believe me?"

She wanted to. She wanted to so much. But then what? What would happen the next time she needed him and he wasn't there? What would happen when he left?

He always left.

"I choose you, Gracie." His eyes were wide, and his hands were trembling around hers. And she realized maybe he was frightened, too. "I love you."

Maybe it doesn't matter what happens next, she thought. *He's here* now.

"I love you, too."

Harper didn't close her eyes. She wanted to see his face as it drew closer, watch his eyes close, his long lashes brush his cheek, his hands cradle her face.

He tasted the same.

She sucked at his lips, stroked the soft skin at the nape of his neck, massaged her fingers through his hair. Everything else fell away, except for the feel of his body pressed to hers.

And the feel of his lips.

Time passed, and they couldn't let go. They had waited too long; they were too hungry for each other.

And then more time passed, and their lips finally parted but their hands stayed clasped as they walked out of the gym and back to the car. They could have stayed there, or found a private place on the side of the road, or driven to that spot behind the ravine where people sometimes went when they needed an escape. It was the desert—there were plenty of places to be alone.

But instead they drove home, and without speaking—without separating—they walked into the backyard and climbed onto the rock, *their* rock, and although the sky was clear and the moon was only a sliver, they never noticed the stars.

They were still there, on the rock, Harper's head on Adam's chest, cradled in Adam's arms, when dawn lit up the sky with a new day. And even then, they might have stayed, happy, entangled, together—were it not for a previous engagement.

"Good morning," Adam whispered, kissing her on the forehead.

She kissed him on the lips. "Good morning. Ready for this?"

"As I'll ever be."

But neither of them moved. They just lay there, side by side, hands clasped. Their caps and gowns waited inside, and soon enough they'd get up, change, pose for proud parents, prepare themselves for everything to end.

It was early. There was still time to kiss. Time to hold each other. Time to savor their beginning.

chapter

13

It's been scientifically proven: Nothing in this universe is more boring than a graduation ceremony. Even when you're the graduate. *Especially* when you're the graduate, sitting in the 104-degree heat, sweating through the robe that only an hour before had made you stop in the mirror and gape at yourself, thinking, *Can this really be me?* The same robe that had made you pause in conversation with friends to think, in amazement, *This is it.* There may have been a moment of gravitas, of sober recognition, before the ceremony began; it may even have leaked into the grand march onto the football field, as the familiar chords of "Pomp and Circumstance" kept strict four-four time and made the whole thing seem like the closing scene of a bad movie.

But by the time the speechifying really got under way, the robe had turned into a portable sweat lodge and the only thing marking the rhythm of the principal's droning was the loud snoring coming from the third row.

Adam grabbed his cap, tilted his head back to get a good look at the cloudless sky, and prayed for rain. He was supposed to be sitting up onstage, the better to accept his award from the athletics department, but he liked it better here, hidden by the crowd, Harper by his side, no one to see when he yawned or made faces or tried to avoid his coach's questioning stare. As the valedictorian rose to start her speech, starting out with some pretentious quote about reaching for the stars, Adam finally gave in to the inevitable. He closed his eyes.

Beth sat at attention, trying not to pretend she didn't care that she wasn't up there in the salutatorian's seat, waiting to deliver her speech and prove to the world that she was . . . well, second best, which was still pretty good. She'd been in the running until October, when everything, including her grades, had overshot the cliff and done a Wile E. Coyote plummet to the bottom. At least she was starting to dig herself out of the hole and walk away.

Reed would have been sitting several rows behind her, if he'd followed the orders about alphabetical seating, which seemed unlikely, since no one but Beth had bothered. Maybe he would have been staring at her—or, more likely, staring blankly, bored and stoned.

But he wasn't there at all.

Adam dozed on Harper's shoulder as the principal droned out the names, waking only to clap for her, and then again to ascend the stage and pick up his own diploma. But Harper listened to every name. Powers, Ramirez, Resnick, Richards, Sambor, Sauer, Segredo . . . Solomon.

Skipping right over it, as if Kaia Sellers had never existed, as if there wasn't an empty chair where she should have been, smoothing down her hair and making snide comments about everything and everyone in her sightline. And there *was* no empty chair, no pause where her name should have been, not even a cheesy memorial that would have made all the posers fake cry while making Harper want to vomit. There was just that split second between Segredo and Solomon, one second for Harper to fill in a silent name and let herself imagine for one last time how things might have been different, how they *should* have been different. Adam squeezed her hand, like he knew, and she realized that maybe she wasn't the only one.

Then came Spiers, and Starrow, and finally Stevens, and as Miranda shook the principal's hand and smiled out at the crowd, Harper pulled herself away from the past, stood up, and cheered.

And Miranda didn't just smile at the crowd, she looked hard, searching for the face she knew wouldn't be there, even as she told herself that he wasn't her problem anymore. He was home, she knew that much. Whether he'd skipped graduation through choice or necessity, she had no idea. He hadn't tried to contact her.

But there was the note, the note that late last night she'd finally set down on her desk, smoothed out, and, knowing that she should probably light it on fire, read slowly and fearfully, and then read again. And again.

It began, *What I should have written in your yearbook.*

It was one page long, handwritten, front and back.

I was too afraid to tell you the truth, it said.

I wasn't good enough for you, it said, further down. *But you made me better.*

I never let myself feel this way about anyone, it said.

I didn't know what to do.

I was scared.

And also: *You're stronger than you look. I'm the opposite.*

It said *I'm sorry* five times.

I want to say please don't hate me, it said. *That would be a very me thing to say.*

But, *Please hate me,* it said.

It said *thank you* once, but it didn't say for what.

The word *love* appeared only once, at the end.

I wish I could have meant this the way you deserved. But I mean it the best way I can:

Love,

Kane.

There was a loud cheer, and a flock of black caps took flight.

It was over.

Harper couldn't keep her hands off his bare skin. It was warm, like something was burning just beneath the tan, taut surface. She pressed her hand flat against his abs, then ran her fingers lightly up his chest, tickling his neck. He laughed, then lunged toward her, nipping playfully at her ear, her nose, and then tickling his fingers across her neck and back until she convulsed in giggles, shaking helplessly in his arms.

It was a secluded spot in the desert, hidden from non-existent passersby by a small grove of Joshua trees, which meant absolute privacy to enjoy themselves—and each other.

As the laughter drifted away, they lay still, spent, tangled up in each other.

"I wish we could stay here all day," Harper mused, kissing his bare shoulder. "And all night . . ."

"You're the one who wanted all the group festivities," Adam reminded her. "I would have been perfectly happy—"

"I don't want Miranda to be alone," she said. "Not tonight."

"I know." He curled himself around her, lightly stroking her bare arm. "It'll be fun."

"Speaking of alone . . . ," she said hesitantly. She'd promised herself that she would do this, but now that the moment had arrived, she wasn't sure she could go through with it. But Harper Grace had never backed away from a challenge. "If you want to bring Beth tonight . . . you should. Invite her along, I mean."

Adam gave her a sharp look. "Are you serious? You want me to bring *Beth*?"

"Of course I don't *want* you to," Harper said, recoiling. "But . . ." She reached for his hand and laced their fingers together. "I'm trying, okay? If you need this, I'm trying to be okay with it."

He raised their linked hands to his lips and kissed her fingertips. "You're amazing," he whispered. "How did we waste so much time?"

Harper winced. It wasn't her favorite topic, not now that she was racing the clock. She'd been waiting for graduation for so long—and now that it was here, all she could think was, *One month, and then he leaves me again.*

"We have time," she murmured, nestling into him, wishing that every inch of their bodies could be in contact at once. "Just not enough."

"Maybe more than you think."

Harper sat up. "Did they push back the date you have to leave?"

"Maybe . . . maybe I'm not going."

"What?"

Adam sat up too, cracking his knuckles one by one as he did when he was bored or nervous. "I'm calling the guy today to give him my decision, and I've been thinking . . ." He shook his head. "Maybe it's not such good idea. It's so far away, and you know me and school." He made a sour-milk face. "Not a perfect match. And you and me, we only just—" He put an arm around her shoulders. "I don't want to leave. Not now."

Everything had already been almost perfect—and now the *almost* had vanished. Without her having to wheedle, manipulate, lie, cheat, beg, or do any of the other things she'd always tried in the past when life had threatened to sweep her in the wrong direction. It had just happened, with no effort whatsoever. Adam was staying true to his word: He was choosing her. It seemed almost too good to be true.

And it is. She didn't want to hear the voice, but it was persistent, and it was loud. It was her own.

"You have to go," she told him, confused by the words coming out of her mouth. Since when had she developed a conscience? And what would this disgusting voice of righteousness have to say in a few months, when she was lying in an empty bed missing Adam, miserable, alone? What would it say when Adam found some nubile, overly flexible, morally challenged Riverside cheerleader to occupy his time while Harper was waiting for his phone call hundreds of miles away?

"You have to go," she said again, pushing away thoughts of the future. "This is too big, it's too much. You can't give it up for me."

"It's not just for you," he protested. "It's, you know, it's far away, and a lot of . . . okay, it's for you. But it's for me, too. I don't want to leave you."

"And I'm not letting you stay," she said, trying to sound tough. "You're not that dumb, Ad. You can't walk away from something like this. This is your future."

"Who are you, my guidance counselor?"

Who was she?

His new girlfriend, who would miss him too much to bear, who deserved more than a few weeks to actually be happy before he ripped her heart out again?

Or his old friend, his best friend, who knew what was right for him—and knew that she couldn't get in the way?

"I'm the one who knows you better than anyone else," Harper said. "That's what you're always saying, right? And I know this is what you really want. This is what you need. You have to go for it."

"Then come with me!"

She could see past the eagerness right through to the desperation, and the knowledge that it wasn't going to happen.

Even so, she let herself imagine it for a moment, just picking up and driving across the desert with him, landing in Riverside, finding an apartment, a part-time job, living in sin (and watching her mother's head explode as a not-so-trivial side benefit), having Adam around every day, every minute, whenever she wanted him, close enough to touch.

She gave herself that one moment to live in the fantasy. And then it was back to real life.

"I can't do that to Miranda," she told him. "We've got plans. And . . . *I've* got plans. I can't just follow you. Even if . . . even though it would be amazing." She tipped her face forward so that their foreheads kissed. "One year. There are vacations, and we can visit each other on the weekends, and . . . maybe it won't be so bad." She wasn't trying to convince him. She was trying to convince herself.

"One year," he echoed, touching her face like he was trying to memorize its shape. "We can do that."

"And after that, if we're still together—"

"We *will* be," he said, with more certainty than she could allow herself. But maybe that was okay. She was sure of only one thing: If it all went wrong again, she would fight for them—and maybe this meant he would fight too.

"I'll miss you," she said, eyes pressed together tightly so that no emotion—or anything else—could leak out.

He touched her lips. "Smile," he said. "I'm not gone yet."

Four weeks. It wasn't enough time. It wasn't fair.

But—she kissed him, hard, and wrapped her body around his—it was better than nothing. And it would have to do.

Don't expect anything, Beth reminded herself, creeping slowly up the path. She clutched the letter in her hands, trying to envision how this would go—how it should go. She could hand it to him, then run away. Or she could ask him to read it while she stood there, watching his face for some hint of understanding. Or maybe she should just set it down on the doorstep and leave without making him face her again.

That was probably the right thing to do, but just this one last time, Beth allowed herself to ignore that. She needed to see him. She needed to explain why she had written the letter—it wasn't because she hoped to excuse herself or even explain herself. She wasn't trying to get him back. She just wanted to help him understand what she'd done to him—and to thank him, for everything he'd done for her. They'd been together for such a short time, but somehow he'd managed to crawl inside her, to *change* her. It was all in the letter—all that, and another apology. Not for the way she'd hurt Kaia, but for the way she'd hurt him.

His father answered the door. At least, Beth assumed it was his father; they'd never met.

"Is Reed here?" she asked.

"You just missed him," the man said.

"Oh." Beth tried not to be too disappointed. "Can I, um, leave this for him?"

The man wiped his hands on his pants, smearing a streak of black grease across the worn denim. He took the letter. "He'll be gone a few months, but I can hold it for him, if you want."

"Gone?" Her voice squeaked. "Gone where?"

The man shrugged. His hair was lighter than Reed's, and gray at the temples, but it was just as curly. "With his band somewhere. They took off in the van, said they were going on tour. Didn't want to hear my opinion on the topic. And I got one."

"Oh."

Don't cry, she told herself. She took the letter back. "Do you have an address or something? Somewhere I can . . ."

But the man shook his head. "Don't know where he went, don't know when he's coming back. Sorry."

Do not cry.

Reed was gone. It was over. Not that it hadn't been over before. Not that he hadn't been gone—but this was different.

Why hadn't he said he was leaving so soon? Beth wondered. When they'd stood there in the dark, all those things going unsaid—if she'd realized that this was one of them, she might have . . .

What? she asked herself bitterly. *What would be different?*

And the answer: *nothing.*

Maybe this was better. Seeing him only reminded her of what she couldn't have. And letting herself believe that he would still be watching out for her, protecting her, jumping in to save her from herself . . . that was just another sign of weakness. And she was done with all that.

She started her car, then hesitated. Adam had invited her out with him—with "us"—for the night. And despite her grounding, it was tempting. No one would want her around, she knew that. Not even Adam. But being hated and ignored might still be easier than spending the night alone, staring into the empty future.

No.

She'd promised herself she would stop making the easy choices. She wouldn't crash Adam's celebration just because she couldn't stand to spend the night alone. So she drove home.

And by the time she got there, she'd almost convinced herself that it didn't matter that Reed was gone for good. Then she saw the van parked at the curb, and knew she'd been lying to herself once again.

He was leaning against it, waiting.

For her.

Beth ran to him, then stopped abruptly when she was about a foot away—knowing that if she went any farther, she wouldn't be able to stop at all.

"Hey," she said, cool and casual.

"Hey."

"Yo, Beth," Fish called, hanging out of the van, a skinny goth girl with blue-streaked hair and black lipstick clinging to him. Something about her looked vaguely familiar. "Did you hear? We're going on tour."

"Gonna be rock stars, baby," Hale said, waving from the driver's seat. He had a goth groupie of his own, almost identical to the first, except that her streaks were purple. She waved as if she knew Beth.

"Tell Harper we say thanks for the advice!" the groupie chirped.

"Yeah, and that she was right. We needed a change. Uh, dude," her friend added. Then, in sync, they turned toward their rock stars and commenced with the PDA.

Reed touched her arm. "Want to walk?"

Beth nodded, and they started slowly down the sidewalk, both looking at the ground.

"So you're leaving?" she asked.

"Yeah. For a while."

"That's great." But she couldn't muster up much enthusiasm.

He shrugged. "We'll see. Could be good, could be . . . well, you know the guys."

"Yeah." She smiled weakly. "Well, good luck, I guess."

"You, too. So . . . you sticking around here for a while?"

The awkwardness was almost physically painful. Beth couldn't believe there had been a time when they'd spent hours together without noticing the time pass. And now they'd been reduced to pitiful small talk? The raw, angry silence between them had almost been better—at least it meant that there was still something between them, that they weren't just strangers with nothing in common except a miserable past.

"For a while," she replied. "I figured I'd take a few classes at State and save up some money, then reapply to Berkeley. I'll do whatever it takes to get in this time." It was the first time she'd said it out loud, and she was surprised to hear that it sounded like a solid plan. For the first time, she began to believe it might work.

"That's cool," he said. She winced at the tone; she knew when he was trying to be polite. "You will."

"Thanks. So . . ." She waited for him to explain why he'd come.

"Yeah. Uh, good luck with all that, I guess."

"You too. With the tour, and everything."

"Beth, before I go . . ." He stopped walking, and she turned, waiting for him to continue. "I didn't want to leave without . . . you know. Saying good-bye."

"I'm glad," she said softly. "I'll miss you."

There was a pause. "I miss *you*," he said. "That's what I wanted to tell you."

She couldn't speak.

"And also . . . I forgive you."

"Reed, you don't have to—"

"No. Just let me—" He shook his head. "I know you didn't mean for it to happen. And . . . I get why you had to lie. Why you thought you had to. I'm not even . . ." He took a step toward her and raised a hand, awkwardly, then dropped it again. "Maybe I'm not even sorry. That you did. The two of us, we . . ."

"It was amazing," she said, and no amount of telling herself not to cry would prevent the tear from dripping out. She wiped it away before he could see. "And I ruined everything."

"No."

"Yes."

"Well . . . okay, yes. But—" He touched her face with the back of his hand, running his nails lightly down her cheek. "It's over. Let it go, okay? I'm trying to. I just—I want you to be happy. Let yourself be happy."

"I want to," she whispered.

Reed glanced back at the van. "I should take off."

She nodded. "How long will you be gone?"

"Don't know. A while."

"I wish . . ."

"Yeah. Me too." He smiled his crooked smile, and then his arms were around her, hugging her tightly, and she leaned against him one last time, pressing her face into his neck and breathing in the rich, deep smell: coffee, cigarettes, and beneath it something warm and sweet, like almonds roasted in honey. "I'm not mad anymore," he said softly, squeezing tighter. "I'm not. I just—I can't be with you. Not after . . . not yet."

"I know."

"Maybe someday," he whispered. "Maybe things will be different."

"Maybe," she breathed, even though they both knew it was a lie. And maybe whatever was between them wouldn't have lasted, anyway. Maybe as time passed, and she'd gotten stronger, she would have remembered herself, and the two of them wouldn't have worked. Maybe. But she didn't believe that, either. She still loved him. She just couldn't have him.

Her maybes were just pretty ways to disguise the truth. There was only one maybe she could cling to: *Maybe* it would be okay. Maybe she would move on, and stand on her own, and let herself be happy.

Maybe it was possible.

"I don't want to let go," she murmured.

"Me neither." But then he did, only a little, enough to see her face, and then he leaned in and kissed her, as softly and tentatively as he had the first time, when he'd been afraid of hurting her and she'd been too weak to push him away. So she'd let him get hurt instead.

This time, she was stronger.

"Good-bye, Reed," she said, still so close, she could feel his lips brushing against hers. And she let him go.

"You sure you want to do this?" Harper asked, hesitating with her finger on the doorbell.

Miranda smiled ruefully. "I don't know about you guys, but I'm kind of partied out."

"Yeah, but there's plenty of other stuff we could do—" Harper began.

"We're doing this," Miranda said firmly.

Harper looked skeptical, but Adam pressed his hand over hers, and the doorbell rang.

Miranda tried to freeze her face in a neutral expression, and waited for the door to open.

"What are you guys doing here?" Kane asked. He looked normal enough, if more casual than usual in jeans and an old T-shirt. "If you came by to lecture me—or threaten me," he added, looking at Harper, "good timing. My dad just left, and we wouldn't want the ranting and raving to let up for more than a few seconds."

"Get over yourself," Harper said, pushing past him into the house. "We're crashing your pity party, Felon Boy. And we brought reinforcements." She nodded at Adam, who pulled a bottle of Champagne out from behind his back.

Miranda didn't say anything, just stood slightly behind the rest of them, listening and waiting. She couldn't quite look at Kane.

"How you doing?" Adam asked, throwing himself on one of the couches.

Kane shrugged. "Out on bail, sporting the latest in felon fashion"—he raised the cuff of his jeans to reveal a black electronic ankle bracelet—"you know, same old, same old."

Miranda still wasn't looking, but she could feel his eyes on her.

"Can I talk to you for a minute?" he asked quietly.

Miranda shrugged. "I guess."

Harper grabbed her wrist. "You need backup?"

"I think I got it," Miranda said, and followed Kane into the kitchen. She realized it was kind of odd, how little time they'd spent in this house while they were dating—not to mention all the years they'd known each other.

I keep people out, he had written in his letter. *It's all I know how to do.*

Miranda leaned against a marble counter. Kane stood across from her, looking uncharacteristically awkward and unsure of himself. He rubbed the back of his neck, fiddled with the cuff of his shirt, then finally spoke. "Miranda, I'm really sorry—"

"You don't have to apologize again," she told him. "I get it, you're sorry."

"It was horrible."

"Unforgivable, really."

"And you must hate me."

"Utterly," she agreed, the corners of her mouth creeping up at the edges. It wasn't because she suddenly found him irresistible, or because standing here facing him she was ready to fall for his charm and forgive his every sin.

That's what she'd been afraid of—it's why she hadn't wanted to come. And why she'd had to come.

But it wasn't happening. She finally met his eyes, and for the first time he wasn't Kane Geary, cool, charismatic, charming Greek god with the perfect body and irresistible smile who could get away with anything. He was just Kane, the guy she'd known forever, the guy who'd made some mistakes. Whatever power over her that he'd once had, it was gone.

And now she let her mouth widen into a smile, because she'd passed her first test. She had faced him, and she was still in control. She was free.

"Miranda, if I could go back, if I could—"

"Save it, Geary." She hopped onto the counter, enjoying the sensation of being above his eye level, rather than several inches below. "You did it, and it sucked, but you did the right thing in the end. If you hadn't—" She shivered, imagining what it would be like if she were the one locked into a metal bracelet, facing court dates, trials, sentencing. . . . "Anyway, thanks for that."

"I should have done it sooner," he said.

"Damn right."

Kane leaned against the counter next to her, his hand next to hers. They didn't touch.

"So what happens next?" she asked.

"Penn State's over," he said, tipping his head back as far as it would go and then expelling a long, angry breath. "Even if they don't revoke my admission, well, let's just say my dad's not going to be shelling out massive amounts of tuition money for me anytime soon. He's not too happy right now."

"I'm sorry." And it was even a little true. "I know how much you wanted to get out of here."

"I still might," he said with a bitter laugh, "if the cops get their way." He sighed. "But it seems like my dad's lawyer's going to get the case kicked. Insufficient evidence, illegal search and seizure, something. I don't know. I haven't really been thinking about it."

Miranda raised an eyebrow. "What else is there to think about?"

He turned toward her, and he didn't have to say it out loud. For once, his eyes actually gave him away.

"Stevens, I . . . you have to know . . . I . . ."

Part of her was tempted to let him keep torturing

himself, blurting out nonsensical phrases in that strangled voice. Maybe if she waited long enough, he would actually choke out a sincere sentiment or two, much as it pained him.

But she didn't need it, not anymore. Besides, sweet and sincere didn't really become him.

"I don't hate you," she said finally, putting him out of his misery. "I'm not even that mad anymore. Promise."

"So I've still got a chance?"

"With me?" Miranda jumped off the counter, laughing. "A fat chance," she said. "Very, very fat. Like sumo wrestler fat."

He smiled wryly. "I had to ask."

"I'm glad you did." And then, like it was nothing, she rose up on her toes and gave him a quick kiss on the lips, allowing herself a split second to remember other, better, longer kisses and everything that had come with them, then stepped back, surprised at how easy it was. "Look me up when you get out on parole," she teased, "and we'll see if you're a changed man."

The famous Kane Geary smirk made its first appearance of the night. "Stranger things have been known to happen, Stevens. You never know."

"Never" was the right word, she told herself, because he'd never change. And she'd never let him back in, or anyone like him. She wouldn't be that stupid again. Whatever he said, now or later, she finally knew better. She'd made herself a promise, and she was sticking to it.

But there was that smile, and those eyes . . . and his letter.

Never, she told herself firmly. *Never again.*

Then again—cue smirk—stranger things have been known to happen.

"So, what are we toasting to?" Kane asked, pouring the champagne into his father's best glasses. "Maybe to not getting sick off this cheap drugstore booze?"

Harper smacked him on the shoulder, not so lightly. "Maybe to the fact that your friends are willing to put up with a soulless sleazebag like you for one more night?"

Kane gave her his sweetest, smarmiest smile. "So you're saying we're friends again? I better go write it down in my diary. I've been so worried about losing my BFF."

She raised an arm to smack him again, but Adam caught it in midswoop and pulled her into his arms. "How about to finally figuring things out," he suggested, giving Harper a knowing smile.

Miranda grinned and raised a glass. "That works for me."

Harper's hands tightened around the glass. She leaned her head back against Adam's chest and watched Miranda stretch out as Kane, for once, watched *Miranda*, darting glances at her when he thought no one was looking. There was an empty glass sitting on the liquor cabinet—*one for Kaia*, she thought, *who should've been here*.

She had known the people in this room for most of her life, and she knew them better than she knew anyone, saw them more than she saw her own parents, day after day, year after year. She knew the way Miranda looked when she was about to sneeze, the arm Kane preferred using when he was trying to tickle his latest conquest, the song Adam hummed to himself when he was working on a

math problem or setting up the perfect three-point shot—
and they knew just as much about her.

And they put up with her anyway.

"It's all over, isn't it?" she said suddenly. "Nothing's
going to be the same after this."

Kane looked at her like she was crazy. "Would you *want*
it to be the same? Do you not remember . . . everything?"

"It hasn't been the best year," Miranda pointed out.

"See, even the nostalgia queen agrees with me," Kane
said.

"It's kind of been the worst." Adam leaned down to kiss
the top of her head. "At least, until recently."

"I know, but . . ."

But it wasn't true. Or, at least, it wasn't the whole
truth. Things had been hard—things had, at times, been
impossible—but no easy fight was worth winning. It
wasn't that she had no regrets; it wasn't that she would
have done it the same way all over again. It wasn't that she
thought it had all worked out for the best. Some mistakes,
you couldn't fix, no matter how much you wanted to.
Some things you couldn't get back.

It wasn't that she had forgotten the year's failures, the
nights she'd lain in bed staring into the dark, willing herself not to cry—and it wasn't even that the triumphs were
so sweet that they overpowered the flavor of defeat. It was
that they had been through so much—too much—and
they had still ended up here, celebrating, victorious.
Together. They had battled and bloodied one another, they
had kept secrets, broken hearts, lied, betrayed, exiled, they
had walked away, said goodbye and sworn it was forever,
and somehow, every time, they had mended, they had

forgiven, they had survived. Some mistakes could never be fixed—some, but not all.

Some people can't be driven away, no matter how hard you try. Some friendships won't break.

"It wasn't the best year," she admitted. "But it had its moments. *We* had our moments."

Kane smirked. "Since when did you become Little Miss Sunshine?"

Harper leaned into Adam, who wrapped his arms around her waist. "Since I got a clue." She pressed her lips together and swallowed hard. *Graduation only meant the end of high school,* she told herself, *not the end of everything.* There was no need to get weepy or to bathe in nostalgic schmaltz. Even if she was surrounded by the only people who'd ever mattered to her; even if this was the beginning of good-bye. She was Harper Grace, and her eyes would stay dry as she raised her glass. Her hand would *not* tremble. And her voice would never break.

"To survival," she said, and it wasn't a suggestion. "Whatever it takes."

Miranda nodded and clinked her glass against Harper's. "And to sticking together."

"Even when we should know better," Kane added, raising an eyebrow.

Clink.

"To never giving up on each other," Adam said.

Clink.

Harper drank last, waiting for the rest of them to tilt their glasses back. She wanted to fix the image in her mind, to remember them celebrating. She wanted to remember them happy. And then she brought her own glass to her lips and tipped it toward her mouth, the fizzy champagne sharp on her tongue and icy cool as it trickled down her throat.

To surviving, she thought, as Adam's arms tightened around her. *To whatever comes next.*

To us.

**Here's a taste of Robin Wasserman's
next novel:**

HACKING HARVARD

"You'll laugh."

"Probably," I admitted.

We were sitting on the edge of the roof, the open dome beneath us and the lights of Boston and Cambridge spread out in every direction.

Eric sighed. "You really want to know?"

"Well, *now* I do," I said, giving him a light shove. "You've built it up too much."

"Fine." There was a long pause. "Batman."

I laughed.

"Shut up!" He tried to shove me back, but I grabbed his arms and wrestled them down. His hands were icy. Our eyes met, and I let go. He was blushing. "I told you you'd laugh."

"You just told me you wanted to be Batman when you grow up," I pointed out. "What was I supposed to do?"

"I tried to give you the normal answer," he complained.

"And you said think outside the box. You said my *dream* job."

"And then *you* said Batman." I started laughing again, letting myself slide backward until I was lying flat on the thin picnic blanket he'd brought along. Even with all the city lights, we could still see the stars.

"Well, not really, not with the costume or anything. And I don't want to live in a cave. But look, he's a millionaire, he's got all these amazing gadgets, he goes out every night and battles the forces of evil, he always gets the hottest—" He stopped abruptly.

"What?"

"Uh, cars," he said quickly. "Very cool cars. You're telling me you wouldn't want a ride in the Batmobile?" He started ticking the advantages off on his fingers. "Cool car, cool toys, cool mission. That's my answer, and I'm sticking to it. Laugh all you want."

I had to admit, it was more interesting than his "normal" answer, something long, complicated, and impressive-sounding about designing affordable computers for the Third World by using microprocessors that . . . well, that's where I'd tuned out.

Batman I could at least understand.

"I just want to . . . I know it sounds stupid, but I want to change the world," he said. "Somehow. Do *something*. You know?"

I knew.

"Okay," he said. "Your turn."

I took a deep breath, watching the dots of light over my head, remembering that when I was a kid, I'd thought every airplane was a falling star.

"When I grow up? My deepest, darkest, most

laugh-worthy desire?" I shrugged. "I don't know. Ballerina? Vampire slayer? Top-secret international government spy?"

"Come on. Really. I told you mine."

What was I supposed to do? Admit that I didn't *have* a plan, laughable or otherwise? That the future seemed flat and finite, like if I tried to sail past the horizon of high school graduation, I might fall off the edge of the world? "Big Dipper," I said instead, pointing west, or at least, the direction I thought was west. "It's the only one I ever learned to recognize."

"Okay, so we can cross astronomer off the career list. That's Orion."

"Oh." Now I was laughing at myself. "As far as I'm concerned, it's just a bunch of random white dots on a black screen. I can never tell where I'm supposed to connect all the stupid imaginary lines. Obviously."

"It's not so hard," he said. "I'll show you."

He lay down next to me, and we stared at the sky. The moon was only a sliver, but I could see his arm, reaching out toward the chains of stars. The night had a reddish glow.

Eric pointed out Cassiopeia, Andromeda, Pisces, the low-hanging bright star that was actually a planet, and, eventually, the Big Dipper. Half of me was paying attention, while the other half was noticing how close our cheeks were to each other, and the fact that if I rolled a little to the left, and he rolled a little to the right, we would collide, face-to-face.

The half-empty bag of Reese's lay between us.

"I don't know why no one comes up here," he said, propping his hands behind his head. "It's such a waste."

Someone came up there. But I decided not to tell him

about the condom wrappers I'd seen in the trash. He was right. It was a waste.

I didn't know what I was doing. I'd forgotten all my plans for the night, and instead, I just lay there, totally relaxed, like all the crap that had been weighing me down was back on the ground, and as long as we stayed up there, in the dark, nothing mattered.

"What are you scared of?" he asked suddenly.

"What?"

"Before. On the bridge. You said you were scared of something, but . . ."

I didn't have to answer. I definitely didn't have to answer *honestly*. I was good at lying.

But I was also tired of it.

So I didn't say anything.

"You're scared of not getting in, aren't you?" he asked quietly.

"What makes you—?"

"I can just see it. You look around like you're trying to picture yourself here, but you don't want to let yourself do it. Like you don't want to count on it, right?"

He said it, I didn't. Just remember that for later. He's the one who brought the whole thing up. All I could do then was tell the truth.

"Yes. That's what I'm scared of." Among other things. "It's like, what if, whatever I do, it's not enough? Everyone's expecting—and even if they say they're not, I know they are, my parents at least, and my teachers, and—what the hell am I supposed to do if something goes wrong? What happens then?"

"Alicia Morgenthal," he said quietly.

I didn't say anything.

"I was in that class, you know," he said. "I saw her. When she—when it happened. I was there."

I hadn't known that.

"You're not like her," he said. "You'd never . . . you're just not."

"You barely know me."

"I know you're different."

I squeezed my eyes shut for a moment, blotting out the stars. When I opened them again, the world seemed too bright. "I bet that's what her friends would have said, too. Before. You think anyone who knew her saw it coming?"

"I didn't," he said softly.

"What?"

"I was her friend. Sort of. I mean, I knew her. And I saw her that night—you know, that last night."

I propped myself up on my elbows and gaped at him, hoping I didn't look too nakedly curious. No one knew where Alicia had disappeared to in the hours between the mailbox stuffed with rejection letters and the calculus class meltdown the next morning. "Saw her where?" I asked, trying to sound casual.

"She came over, and she . . ." He shook his head. "She didn't tell me about, you know, the rejections. She didn't really talk at all. She just . . . I should have known. I should have known something was up."

"How could you, if she didn't say anything?"

"Because she—" Eric broke off abruptly, then contorted his face into a fake smile. "It doesn't matter."

I wanted to know more; I *needed* to know more. But I didn't want to push. So I lay back down and stared at the sky, waiting.

"None of it has anything to do with you," Eric finally said. "*You'll* get in somewhere great."

"Unless I don't." He couldn't understand. He'd been working for some professor at MIT for the past four years. They were probably begging him to go there. The first day of freshman year they'd probably send a limo and roll out a red carpet. "There's nothing I can do about it, one way or another. I have no control."

"And you hate that most of all."

So he got me. So what? It didn't mean anything. I wasn't too hard to figure out. "I guess."

He didn't try to argue me into admitting that it didn't matter where I got in. And he didn't lie and say it would all work out the way I wanted it to. He didn't even look at me. When I glanced over, he was still staring up at the stars. But he moved his hand just a little to the right, until it was resting on top of mine. He wasn't holding it—he wasn't even pressing down. He was just touching it, as lightly as he'd touched my arm by the telescope.

"I'm sorry," he said.

"It's not like you did anything."

"Lex, there's something I should . . ." His voice faded out.

I turned onto my side, and so did he. Our faces were almost touching. I'd only ever been this close to one other guy. Jeff had been taller than Eric and better built, his eyes hadn't been as close together, he hadn't worn glasses, he hadn't had that crooked front tooth or a dimple when he smiled, his lips hadn't been so thin.

And I had never wanted to kiss him this much.

I hadn't stared at Jeff's lips wondering how they would

feel and what they would taste like. Jeff always tasted like spearmint.

Why was I thinking about Jeff when I was staring at Eric?

Gazing. I was *gazing* at Eric, there was no other word for it—moonlight, whispered secrets, and *gazing*. It wasn't the kind of moment I'd expected someone like me to have. Especially not with someone like him.

"Eric . . ." I could see the broad contours of his face, but no more than that. It was too dark to read his expression. I wondered if he could see mine.

Kiss me, I thought, trying to force the words out of my head and into his. Someone was going to have to make a move. And it wasn't going to be me.

He brushed a piece of hair out of my face. He smiled, then opened his lips a little, as if he was about to say something but was pausing, holding the words back. This was it. Sometimes life really is like the movies, and even without a script to follow, you just know.

I knew.

He closed his eyes, leaned in . . .

And I rolled away. Sat up. Jumped to my feet. "I have a curfew," I lied. "We should really start heading back."

About the Author

Robin Wasserman enjoys writing about high school—but wakes up every day grateful that she doesn't have to relive it. She recently abandoned the beaches and boulevards of Los Angeles for the chilly embrace of the East Coast, as all that sun and fun gave her too little to complain about. She now lives and writes in New York City, which she claims to love for its vibrant culture and intellectual life. In reality, she doesn't make it to museums nearly enough, and actually just loves the city for its pizza, its shopping, and the fact that at 3 a.m. you can always get anything you need—and you can get it delivered.

You can find out more about what she thinks of New York, L.A., books, shopping, pizza, life, the universe, and everything else at www.robinwasserman.com.